ANOTHER
VIEW

OTHER DELL BOOKS BY
ROSAMUNDE PILCHER

The Day of the Storm
The Empty House
The End of Summer
The Shell Seekers
Sleeping Tiger
Snow in April
Under Gemini
Wild Mountain Thyme

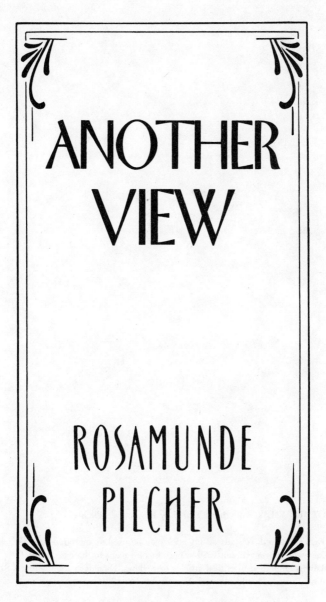

ANOTHER VIEW

ROSAMUNDE PILCHER

St. Martin's Press

ISBN: 0-440-20251-5

Printed in the United States of America

In Paris, in February, the sun was shining. At Le Bourget Airport, it gleamed coldly from an ice blue sky, and this was reflected, with much dazzle, from the runways, still wet after a night's rain. From inside, the day looked inviting, and they had been tempted out on to the terrace, only to discover that the bright sun held no real warmth and the gay breeze that blew the wind socks out at right angles had an edge to it like a knife. Defeated, they withdrew to the restaurant to wait for Emma's flight to be called, and sat now, at a small table, drinking black coffee and smoking Christopher's Gauloises cigarettes.

Unselfconscious, absorbed in each other, they nevertheless attracted a certain amount of attention. This was inevitable, for they made an arresting pair. Emma was tall and very dark. Her hair, worn back off her forehead and held in

1

place by a tortoiseshell band, fell in a straight black tassel to below her shoulder-blades. Her face was not beautiful—it was too clearly boned and strongly built for beauty, with a straight nose, and a square and determined chin. But these features were redeemed and given much charm by large and unexpectedly grey-blue eyes, and a wide mouth, which, although it was quite capable of drooping disconsolately if she did not get her own way, could grin, from ear to ear, like a boy's, when she was happy. She was happy now. She wore, on this cold bright day, a bitter green trouser suit and a white polo-necked sweater that made her face look very brown, but her sophisticated appearance was off-set by the mass of luggage with which she was surrounded, and which appeared, to the casual passerby, to have been salvaged from some disastrous act of God.

It was, in fact, the accumulation of six years of living abroad, but no one was to know this. Three suitcases, at enormous expense, had already been checked in. But there was still a canvas grip, a Prisunic paper carrier sprouting long French loaves, a basket bulging with books and records, a raincoat, a pair of ski-boots and an enormous straw hat.

Christopher surveyed it all, speculating, in a detached and un-bothered fashion, as to how it was all going to be conveyed into the aeroplane.

"You could wear the hat and the ski-boots and the raincoat. That would make three less things to carry."

"I've already got a pair of shoes on, and the hat would blow off. And the raincoat's disgusting. I look like a displaced person in it. I can't think why I bothered to bring it at all."

"I'll tell you why. Because it will be raining in London."

"It may not be."

"It always is." He lit another Gauloise from the stub of the first. "Another good reason for staying in Paris with me."

"We've had this out a hundred times. And I'm going back to England."

He grinned without rancour. He had been teasing her. When he smiled, his yellow-flecked eyes slanted upwards at the corners, and this, combined with his lanky, idle body, gave him a curiously feline appearance. His clothes were colourful, casual, faintly Bohemian. Narrow cord trousers, battered chukka boots, a blue cotton shirt worn over a yellow sweater, and a suède jacket, very old and shiny about the elbows and the collar. He looked French, but in fact he was as English as Emma, and even related to her in a tenuous way, for, years ago, when Emma was six and Christopher ten, her father, Ben Litton, had married Hester Ferris, Christopher's mother. The arrangement had lasted, with only the smallest degree of success, for eighteen months, before it finally fell apart, and now Emma remembered it as the only time in her life when she had ever known anything vaguely approaching an ordinary family life.

It was Hester who had insisted on buying the cottage at Porthkerris. Ben had owned a studio there for a number of years, since long before the war, but its conveniences were non-existent, and after one look at the squalor in which she was expected to live Hester went straight out and acquired two fisherman's cottages, which she proceeded, with taste and charm, to convert. Ben was disinterested in any such activity, so it became very much Hester's house, and it was she who insisted on a kitchen that would work, and a boiler that would heat water, and a big fireplace blazing with drift-wood, a heart to their home, a focal point around which the children could gather.

Her intentions were splendid, her methods of carrying them out not so successful. She tried to make allowances for Ben. She had married a genius, and she knew his reputation and she was prepared to turn a blind eye to his love affairs, his disreputable companions and his attitude towards money. But in the end, as so often happens in quite ordinary marriages, she was defeated by the small things. By meals, forgotten and uneaten. By trivial bills left unpaid for months. By the fact that Ben preferred to drink in the local pub, rather than in a civilized fashion, at home, with her. She was defeated by his refusal to have a telephone, to own a car; by the stream of apparent derelicts whom he invited to sleep on her sofa; and finally by his total inability to show at any time any sort of affection.

She left him at last, taking Christopher with her, and sued almost immediately for a divorce. Ben was delighted to let her have it. He was delighted, too, to see the back of the small boy. The two of them had never got on. Ben was jealous of his male priority, he liked to be the only man of importance in his household, and Christopher, even at ten years old, was an individual who refused to be ignored. Despite all Hester's efforts, this antagonism endured. Even the boy's good looks, which Hester truly believed would charm Ben's painter's eye, had the very opposite effect, and when Hester tried to persuade Ben to do a portrait of him, he refused.

After their departure, life at Porthkerris slid easily back into its old seamy routine. Emma and Ben were cared for by a series of messy females, either models or student painters, who moved into and through and out of Ben Litton's life with the monotonous regularity of a well-ordered cinema queue. The only thing they had in common was an adulation of Ben, and a lofty disregard for housekeeping. They took as little notice of Emma as possible, but, in fact, she did not miss Hester as much as people thought she would. She had become weary—as Ben was—of being organised, and perpetually buttoned into clean clothes, but Christopher's going left a great void in her life which refused to be filled. For a little, she had mourned for him, tried to write him letters, but had not dared to ask Ben for his address. Once, in the desperation of loneliness, she ran away to find him. This entailed walking to the station and trying to buy a ticket to London, which seemed as good a place as any to look for him. But she had only one and ninepence in the world, and the stationmaster, who knew her, had taken her into his office which smelt of paraffin lamps and the black railway coal he burnt in his grate, and had given her a cup of tea out of an enamel pot, and walked her home. Ben was working, and had not noticed her absence. She never tried to look for Christopher again.

When Emma was thirteen, Ben was offered a teaching fellowship at the University of Texas for two years, which, without thought of Emma, he instantly accepted. There was a small hiatus while Emma's future was discussed. When taxed with the question of his daughter, he announced that he would simply take her to Texas with him, but someone— probably Marcus Bernstein—persuaded Ben that she would be better off away from him, and she was sent to a school in Switzerland. She stayed in Lausanne for three years—never returning to England, and then went to Florence to study Italian and Renaissance Art, for another year. At the end of this time, Ben was in Japan. When she suggested that she should join him, he replied by telegram. ONLY SPARE BED OC- CUPIED BY CHARMING GEISHA GIRL WHY DONT YOU TRY LIVING IN PARIS.

Philosophically, for she was now seventeen and life was no longer surprising, Emma did as he suggested. She found herself a job with a family called Duprés who lived in a tall scholarly house in St. Germain. The father was a Professor of Medicine, and the mother a teacher. Emma cared for their three well-behaved children, taught them English and Ital- ian, and took them, in August, to the modest family villa at

La Baule, and all the time waited patiently until Ben should return to live in England. He stayed in Japan for eighteen months, and when he did return it was by way of the United States, where he spent a month in New York. Marcus Bernstein flew out to meet him there, and it was typical that Emma learned the reason for this reunion, not from Ben himself, nor even from Leo, who was her usual source of information, but from a long and fully illustrated article in the French *Réalités*, which dealt with a newly built Museum of Fine Arts in Queenstown, Virginia. This museum was a memorial created by his widow, to a rich Virginian called Kenneth Ryan, and the opening of the Art Section was to be a retrospective exhibition of the paintings of Ben Litton, ranging from his pre-war landscapes, right through to his latest abstractionisms.

Such an exhibition was an honour and a tribute, but inevitably suggested a painter to be revered, a Grand Old Man of the arts. Emma, studying one of the photographs of Ben, all angles and contrasts, dark-tanned skin and jutting chin and snowy hair, wondered how he felt about such veneration. He had been a rebel all his life against convention, and she could not imagine him tamely submitting to being a Grand Old anything.

"But what a man!" said Madame Duprés, when Emma showed her the photograph. "He is very attractive."

"Yes," said Emma, and sighed, because that had always been the trouble.

With Marcus, he returned to London in January, and went straight back to Porthkerris to paint. This was confirmed by a letter from Marcus. The day the letter arrived, Emma went to Madame Duprés and gave in her notice. They tried to coax, cajole, bribe her into changing her mind, but she was adamant. She had scarcely seen her father for six years. It was time they got to know each other again. She was going back to Porthkerris, to live with him.

In the end, because they had no option, they agreed to letting her go. Her flight was booked, and she started to pack, throwing out some of the accumulated possessions of six years, and cramming the rest into a variety of battered and much-travelled suitcases. But even these were sadly inadequate, and Emma was eventually driven to going out and buying herself a basket, a huge French marketing basket that would accommodate the number of awkwardly-shaped objects that refused to go into anything else.

It was a grey and cold afternoon, two days before she was due to fly home. Madame Duprés was at home, so Emma, explaining her errand, left the children with her, and went out alone. To her surprise, she found that it was raining, lightly, in a chill drizzle. The cobbled pavements of the narrow street shone with wet, and the tall bleached houses stood quiet and closed against the murk, like faces which give nothing away. From the river a tug hooted, and a solitary gull hung, high above, in the mist, screaming dismally. The illusion of Porthkerris was suddenly more real than the reality of Paris. The resolve to return, which had for so long been in the back of her mind, was crystallised now into the impression that she was already there.

This street would lead—not to the busy Rue St. Germain, but out onto the harbour road, and it would be flood tide, the harbour full of grey sea and bobbing boats, and a heavy swell running out beyond the north pier, the Atlantic crested with white horses. And there would be familiar smells—fish from the market, and hot saffron buns from the baker's; and all the little summer shops would be shuttered and closed for the season. And back at the studio Ben would be working, hands mittened against the cold, the brilliance of his palette a scream of colour against the sweep of grey cloud that was framed by his towering north window.

She was going home. In two days, she would be there. The rain was wet on her face and all at once she felt that she could not wait, and this sense of happy urgency made her run, and she ran all the way to the little épicerie in the Rue St. Germain, where she knew she would be able to buy the basket.

It was a tiny shop, fragrant with fresh bread and garlic-flavoured sausage meat, with onions strung like white beads from the ceiling, and jars of wine, which the local workmen bought by the litre. The baskets hung at the door, strung together and suspended by a single piece of rope. Emma did not dare untie it and choose herself a basket in case the whole lot fell to the pavement, so she went into the shop to find someone to do it for her. There was only the fat woman with the mole on her face, and she was busy with a customer, so Emma waited. The customer was a young man, fair haired, his raincoat streaked with damp. He was buying a long loaf and a pat of country butter. Emma eyed him and decided that, from the back at least, he looked attractive.

"*Combien?*" he said.

The fat woman did a sum with a stub of pencil. She told him. He felt in his pocket and paid, turned, smiled at Emma and made for the door.

And there he stopped. With his hand against the edge of the door, he swung slowly around, to take a second look. She saw the amber eyes, the slow, incredulous smile.

The face was the same, the familiar, boy's face on the unfamiliar man's body. With the illusion of Porthkerris so near and so strong, it seemed that he was simply an extension of that illusion, a figment of her own highly-stimulated imagination. This was not him. This could not be . . .

She heard herself say "Christo," and it was the most

8

natural thing in the world to call him by the name that only
she had ever used. He said, quietly, "I simply don't believe
it," and then he dropped his parcels and held out his arms
and Emma fell into them, pressed close against the shiny,
wet front of his raincoat.

They had two days to spend together. Emma told Madame Duprés, "My brother is in Paris, " and Madame, who
was kind-hearted, and had, anyway, resigned herself to being without Emma, set Emma free to spend them with
Christopher. They used up these two days in slowly walking
the streets of the city; hanging over the bridges to watch the
barges slip away below them, bound for the south and the
sun; sitting in the thin sunshine and drinking coffee at the
small, round iron tables, and when it rained, taking refuge in
Notre Dame or the Louvre, perched on the stairs beneath
the Winged Victory and always talking. They had so much to
ask and so much to tell. She learned that Christopher, after a
number of false starts, had decided to become an actor. This
was much against his mother's wishes—after eighteen
months of Ben Litton she had had enough of artistic temper-
aments to last her for the rest of her life—but he had stuck
to his guns and even managed to get a scholarship to
R.A.D.A. He had worked for two years in a repertory theatre
in Scotland, had moved, unsuccessfully, to London, done a
little television work, and then had been diverted by an invitation from an acquaintance, whose mother owned a house
in St. Tropez.

"St. Tropez in the winter?" Emma could not help asking.

"It was then or never. We'd never have been offered it
in the summer."

"But wasn't it cold?"

"Freezing. Never stopping raining. And when the wind
blew all the shutters rattled. It was like some ghastly film."

In January he had returned to London to see his agent, and had been offered a twelve-month contract with a small repertory company in the south of England. It was not the sort of work he wanted, but it was better than nothing, and he was running out of money, and it was not too far from London. The job, however, did not start until the beginning of March, and so he had returned to France, finished up in Paris, and finally met Emma. Now, it irked him that she was returning so soon to England, and did everything he could to make her change her mind, postpone her flight, stay in Paris with him. But Emma was adamant.

"You don't understand. This is something that I have to do."

"It's not even as though the old boy asked you to go. You're just going to get in his way, and interfere with all his amorous adventures."

"I never have before—interfered, I mean." She laughed at his stubborn expression. "Anyway, there's no point my staying, if you're coming back to England next month."

He made a face. "Wish I wasn't. That lousy little theatre at Brookford. I shall get lost in the jungle of fortnightly rep. Besides, I'm not due there for two weeks. Now if you would only stay in Paris . . ."

"No, Christo."

"We could rent a tiny attic. Think of all the fun we could have. Bread and cheese every night for supper and lots of rough red wine."

"No, Christo."

"Paris in the Spring . . . blue skies and blossom and all that rot?"

"It isn't spring yet. It's still winter."

"Were you always so unco-operative?"

But still she would not agree to staying, and in the end he admitted defeat. "Very well, if I can't persuade you to keep me company, I shall simply behave in a very well-bred and British way, and come and see you on to your plane."

"That would be perfect."

"It's very self-sacrificing of me. I hate saying good-byes."

Emma agreed with this. Sometimes, it felt as if she had been saying goodbye to people all her life, and the sound of a train moving out of a station, gathering speed, was enough to reduce her to tears. "But this goodbye is different."

"How is it different?" he wanted to know.

"It isn't really goodbye. It's au revoir. A stepping stone between two hullos."

"My mother and your father are not going to approve."

"It doesn't matter if they approve or not," said Emma. "We've found each other again. For the moment, that's all that matters."

Above them, the loudspeakers gave a click, began to speak with a feminine voice.

"Ladies and gentlemen. Air France announce the departure of their flight Number 402 for London . . ."

"That's me," said Emma.

They stubbed out their cigarettes, stood up, began to gather in the baggage. Christopher took the canvas grip and the Prisunic paper carrier, and the great bulging basket. Emma slung the raincoat over her shoulder, carried her handbag, the ski-boots and the hat.

Christopher said, "I wish you'd wear the hat. It really would complete your ensemble."

"It would blow off. Not to say look funny."

They went downstairs, crossed the expanse of shining floor towards the barrier where a small queue of passengers was already forming.

"Emma, are you going down to Porthkerris to-day?"

"Yes, I'll get the first train I can."

"Have you got any money? Pounds, shillings and pence, I mean?"

She had not thought of this. "No. But it doesn't matter. I'll cash a cheque somewhere."

They joined the queue behind a British business man who carried only his passport and a slim briefcase. Christopher leaned forward.

"Oh, sir, I wonder if you could help."

The man swung round, and found to his surprise Christopher's face only inches from his own. Christopher was wearing his sincere expression. "I am sorry, but we're in rather a predicament. My sister's returning to London, she's not been home for six years, and she has such a lot of hand luggage, and she's only just recovered from a serious operation . . ."

Emma remembered Ben saying that Christopher never told a small lie if he could get away with a bigger one. Looking at him as he came out with this outrageous fabrication, she decided that he had chosen his career wisely. He was a wonderful actor.

The business man, thus approached, could make no excuse.

"Well, yes, I suppose . . ."

"It's more than kind of you . . ." The canvas grip and the carrier with the bread went under one arm, the basket in the other along with the slim brief case. Emma felt sorry for him.

"It's just till we get onto the plane . . . it is so kind of you, and you see my brother isn't coming with me . . ."

The queue moved forward, they had reached the barrier.

"Goodbye, darling Emma," said Christopher.

"Goodbye, Christo." They kissed. A brown hand whipped away her passport, riffled the pages, stamped it.

"Goodbye."

They were divided by the barrier, by the formalities of the French government, by other travellers, surging forward.

"Goodbye."

She would have liked him to wait and see her safely onto the plane, but even as she waved, flapping the sun hat, he had turned, and was walking away from her, the light shining on his hair, and his hands buried deep in the pockets of his leather coat.

2

In London, in February, it was raining. It had started to rain at seven o'clock in the morning, and it had rained without ceasing ever since. By half-past eleven only a handful of people had visited the exhibition, and those enthusiasts, one suspected, had simply come in order to get out of the rain. They shed wet raincoats and dripping umbrellas, and stood around, bemoaning the weather before they had even bought themselves a catalogue.

At eleven-thirty, the man came in to buy a picture. He was an American, staying at the Hilton, and he asked to see Mr. Bernstein. Peggy, the receptionist, took the card which he proffered, asked him politely if he would mind waiting for a moment, and then came through to the office to speak to Robert.

"Mr. Morrow, there's an American outside by the name

14

of . . ." she glanced at the card. "Lowell Cheeke. He was here a week ago, and Mr. Bernstein showed him the Ben Litton of the deer, and thought he was going to buy it, but he went off without making up his mind. Said he wanted to mull it over."

"Have you told him Mr. Bernstein's in Edinburgh?"

"Yes, but he can't wait. He's going back to the States the day after to-morrow."

"I'd better see him," said Robert.

He stood up, and while Peggy went to open the door and invite the American in, did a swift spring-clean of his desk, squaring some letters, emptying the ash tray into the wastepaper basket and shoving the basket under the desk with the toe of his shoe.

"Mr. Cheeke," said Peggy, announcing the visitor like a well-trained parlourmaid.

Robert came around the desk to shake hands.

"How do you do, Mr. Cheeke? I'm Robert Morrow, Mr. Bernstein's partner. I am sorry, I'm afraid he's in Edinburgh to-day, but perhaps I could help you . . . ?"

Lowell Cheeke was a short, powerful-looking individual in a dacron raincoat and a narrow-brimmed hat. Both of these were very wet, indicating that Mr. Cheeke had not arrived in a taxi. He began divesting himself, with Robert's help, from these sodden garments, and revealed an uncrushable navy blue terylene suit and a pin-striped nylon shirt. He wore rimless spectacles and behind them his eyes were cool and grey, and it was impossible to assess any sort of potential either financial or artistic.

"Thank you very much . . ." said Mr. Cheeke. "What a terrible morning . . ."

"It doesn't look as though it's going to let up either . . . A cigarette, Mr. Cheeke?"

15

"No, thank you, I no longer smoke." He coughed self-consciously. "My wife made me give it up."

They grinned at this female idiosyncrasy. The grin did not reach Mr. Cheeke's eyes. He reached for a chair and settled himself into it, hitching a polished black shoe across his knee. He already looked very much at home.

"I was in here a week ago, Mr. Morrow, and Mr. Bernstein showed me a painting by Ben Litton—your receptionist probably told you."

"Yes, she did, the deer painting."

"I'd like to see it again if I may. I'm returning to the States the day after to-morrow, and I have to make up my mind."

"But of course . . . !"

The picture waited for Mr. Cheeke's decision, resting, where Marcus had left it, against the wall of the office. Robert drew the padded easel into the centre of the room, turned it towards the light, and gently lifted the Ben Litton into position. It was a large picture, an oil of three deer in a forest. Light filtered through the barely-suggested branches, and the artist had used a quantity of white which gave the work an ethereal quality. But its most interesting feature was the fact that it had been painted, not on stretched canvas, but on jute, and the coarser weave of this textile had blurred the artist's brush, like the outlines of an action photograph taken at high speed.

The American swung his chair into position, and turned the cold beam of his spectacles onto the painting. Discreetly, Robert removed himself to the back of the room so as not to obtrude in any way upon Mr. Cheeke's own assessment, and his own view of the painting was obscured by the round crew-cut head of his potential customer. Personally, he liked the picture. He was not a fan of Ben Litton's. He thought his work affected and not always easy to understand—a reflection, perhaps of the artist's own personality—but this swift sylvan impression was a thing to be looked at and lived with and never tired of.

Mr. Cheeke got out of his chair, moved up to the painting, examined minutely, backed away once more, and finished up leaning against the edge of Robert's desk.

"Why do you suppose, Mr. Morrow," he said, without turning round, "that Litton was inspired to paint it on burlap?"

The word burlap made Robert want to laugh. He longed to say irreverently, *Probably had an old sack lying around* but Mr. Cheeke did not look as though he would appreciate irreverence. Mr. Cheeke was here to spend money—always a serious business. Robert decided then that he was buying the Litton as an investment, and he hoped it would pay him off.

He said, "I'm afraid I have no idea, Mr. Cheeke, but it does give a most unusual quality to the work."

Mr. Cheeke turned his head to send Robert a cold smile over his shoulder.

"You are not as well informed on such aspects as Mr. Bernstein."

"No," said Robert. "I'm afraid I'm not."

Mr. Cheeke relapsed once more into contemplation. The silence settled and lasted. Robert's own concentration had begun to wander. Small sounds intruded. The ticking of his own wrist watch. A murmur of voices from the other side of the door. The thunderous rumble, like distant surf, that was Piccadilly traffic.

The American sighed gustily. He began to feel in his pockets, one by one, searching for something. A handkerchief, perhaps. Some change for his taxi ride back to the Hilton. His attention had strayed. Robert had not convinced him that the Litton was worth buying. He was going to make some excuse and go away.

But Mr. Cheeke was simply searching for his pen. When he turned round, Robert saw that he already held his cheque book in the other hand.

Their business finally completed, Mr. Cheeke relaxed. He became quite human and even took off his glasses and stowed them away in a tooled leather case. He accepted the offer of a drink, and he and Robert sat for a little, with two glasses of sherry, and talked about Marcus Bernstein and Ben Litton, and the two or three paintings which Mr. Cheeke had purchased on his last visit to London, with which to form, with his latest acquisition, the nucleus of a small private collection. Robert told him about the retrospective Ben Litton exhibition which was being held in Queenstown, Virginia, in April, and Mr. Cheeke made a note of it in his diary, and then they both stood up, and Robert helped Mr. Cheeke into his raincoat, and gave him his hat, and they shook hands.

"I've enjoyed meeting you, Mr. Morrow, and doing business with you."

"I hope we'll see you next time you come to London."

"Most certainly I shall pay you a visit . . ."

Robert held the door open and they moved out into the gallery. Bernstein's were showing, that fortnight, a collection of bird and animal paintings by an obscure South American with an unpronounceable name, a man of humble origins, who had somehow, sometime, incredibly, taught himself to paint. Marcus had met him last year in New York, had been instantly impressed by his work, and invited him then and there to stage a London exhibition. Now, his brilliant pictures lined the straw-green walls of the Bernstein Gallery and on this gloomy morning seemed to fill the room with the verdancy and sunshine of a more salubrious climate. The critics had loved him. Since the exhibition opened ten days ago, the gallery had never once been empty, and within twenty-four hours there was not a picture that had not been sold.

At this moment, however, there were only three people in the gallery. One of them was Peggy, neat and unobtrusive behind her kidney-shaped desk, busy with the proofs of a new catalogue. Another was a black-hatted man, stooped as a crow, doing a slow round of inspection. The last was a girl, who sat, facing the office door, on the circular buttoned sofa in the middle of the room. She wore a bright green trouser suit and was surrounded by luggage, and appeared to have wandered into Bernstein's under the mistaken impression that it was the waiting-room of a railway station.

Robert, with considerable self-possession, managed to behave as if she was not there. Together he and Mr. Cheeke moved across the thick carpet towards the main door, Robert's head bent to catch the last of Mr. Cheeke's small talk. The glass doors opened and swung shut behind them, and they were swallowed into the gloom of the dismal morning.

Emma Litton said, "Is that Mr. Morrow?"

Peggy looked up. "That's right."

Emma was not used to being ignored. The single swift glance had made her feel uncomfortable. She wished that Marcus was not in Edinburgh. She crossed her legs and then uncrossed them again. From outside came the sound of the departing taxi. In a moment, the glass door opened, once more, and Robert Morrow came back into the gallery. He did not make any comment, simply put his hands in his pockets, and calmly regarded Emma and her attendant chaos.

She decided that she had never, in her life, seen a man who looked less like an art dealer. His was the sort of face that, groggy and unshaven, is helped from a small sailboat at the end of a single-handed circumnavigation; or, darkly goggled, looks down from the peak of a previously unconquered mountain. But here, in the precious and rarefied atmosphere of the Bernstein galleries, he did not fit at all. He was very tall, wide-shouldered, long-legged; all this emphasised—and yet made incongruous—by his smoothly-tailored dark grey suit. In his youth his hair might have been red, but the years had tamed it to a tawny brown, and in contrast his grey eyes seemed pale as steel. He had high cheek-bones and a long, stubborn jaw, and she was diverted by the discovery that such a collection of features could be so attractive, and then remembered that Ben always averred that the character of a man lies, not in his eyes, where emotions are fleeting and can always be masked, but in the physical shape of his mouth, and this man's mouth was wide, with a jutting lower lip, and looked now as though it was trying, hard, not to laugh.

The silence became uncomfortable. Emma tried a smile. She said "Hello!"

For enlightenment, Robert Morrow turned to Peggy. Peggy was amused. "This young lady wants to see Mr. Bernstein."

He said, "I am sorry, he's in Edinburgh."

"Yes, I know, so I've been told. The thing is, I only wanted him to cash me a cheque." He looked more puzzled than ever. Emma decided it was time to explain. "I'm Emma Litton. Ben Litton's my father."

His puzzlement cleared. "But why on earth didn't you say so? I am sorry, I had no idea." He came forward. "How do you do . . ."

Emma stood up. The straw hat, which had been on her knee, floated to the carpet and lay there, adding to the confusion which she had already wrought to the elegantly designed room.

They shook hands. "I . . . there wasn't any reason why you should know who I was. And I'm terribly sorry about all this stuff, but you see I haven't been home for six years, so there's bound to be quite a lot."

"Yes, I can see that."

Emma was embarrassed. "If you can just cash me a cheque, I'll take it all out of your way again. I only want enough to get back to Porthkerris. You see, I forgot to get any sterling when I was in Paris, and I've run out of travellers' cheques."

He frowned. "But how did you get this far? From the airport, I mean?"

"Oh." She had already forgotten. "Oh, there was a kind man on the plane, he helped me to carry my stuff on, and off again at London, and he lent me a pound. I'll have to send it back. I've got his address here . . . somewhere." She felt vaguely in pockets, but could not find the man's card. "Well, anyway, I've got it somewhere." She smiled again, hoping to disarm him.

"And when are you going down to Porthkerris?"

"There's a train at twelve-thirty, I think."

He glanced at his wrist watch. "You've missed that. When's the next?"

Emma looked blank. Peggy broke into the conversation in her usual polite and practical fashion. "I think there's one at two-thirty, Mr. Morrow, but I can check."

"Yes, do that, Peggy. Would the two-thirty be all right for you?"

"Yes, of course. It doesn't matter what time I arrive."

"Is your father expecting you?"

"Well, I wrote him a letter and told him I was coming. But that doesn't mean he's *expecting* me . . ."

He smiled at this. "Yes. Well . . ." He glanced at his watch again. It was twelve fifteen. Peggy was already on the telephone, inquiring about train times. His eyes returned to the turmoil of suitcases. In a feeble effort to improve the situation, Emma stooped and picked up her sun hat.

He said, "I think the best thing would be to get all this out of the way . . . we'll pile it up in the office, and then . . . Have you had anything to eat?"

"I had some coffee at Le Bourget."

"If you catch the two-thirty, there's time for me to give you lunch before you go."

"Oh, you don't have to bother."

"It's no bother. I have to eat anyway and you might as well eat with me. Come along now."

He picked up two of the suitcases, and led the way into the office. Emma gathered up as much as she could carry, and followed him. The deer painting was still on the stand, and she saw it at once and was diverted.

"That's one of Ben's."

"Yes, I just sold it . . ."

"To the little man in the raincoat? It's good, isn't it?" She continued to admire it, while Robert toted the remainder of her luggage. "Why did he paint it on sacking?"

"You'd better ask him when you see him to-night."

She turned and grinned at him over her shoulder. "Influenced, do you think, by the Japanese school?"

"I wish," said Robert, "I'd thought of saying that to Mr. Cheeke. Now, are you ready for lunch?"

He took an enormous black umbrella out of a stand, and stood aside for Emma to go out through the door ahead of him, and they left Peggy to hold the fort, sitting in a gallery restored once more to its usual ordered calm, and they went out into the rain and walked together, beneath the black

umbrella, shouldering their way through the lunch-hour jos-
tle of Kent Street, London, W.I.

He took her to Marcello's where he normally lunched if
he was not expected to entertain some important expense-
account customer. Marcello was an Italian who ran a small
upstairs restaurant, two streets from Bernstein's, and a table
was perpetually reserved for either Marcus or Robert, or
both of them, on the odd occasion when they were able to
lunch together. It was a modest table, in a quiet corner, but
to-day when Robert and Emma came up the stairs, Marcello
took one look at her, with her long tassel of black hair, and
her green trouser suit, and suggested that they might prefer
to sit in the window.

Robert was amused. "Would you like to sit in the window?" he asked Emma.

"Where do you usually sit?" He indicated the small
corner table. "Well, why don't we just sit there?"

Marcello was charmed by her. He led the way to the
smaller table, held Emma's chair for her, gave them each an
enormous menu written in dubious purple ink and went to
fetch two glasses of Tio Pepe while they decided what they
were going to eat.

Robert said, "My stock with Marcello will have gone
up. I don't think I've ever brought a girl here for lunch."

"Who do you usually bring?"

"Just myself. Or Marcus."

"How is Marcus?" . . . her voice was warm.

"He's well. He'll be sorry to have missed you, I know."

"It's my fault. I should have written and told him I was
coming. But as you've probably realised, we Littons aren't
very good at letting anybody know about anything."

"But you knew Ben had gone back to Porthkerris."

"Yes. Marcus wrote and told me that. And I know all
about the retrospective exhibition, because I read an article

on it in *Réalités.*" She smiled wryly. "Being the daughter of a famous father does have some compensations. Even if he never does anything except send telegrams, you can usually read up what is happening to him in some paper or other."

"When did you last see him?"

"Oh," she shrugged. "Two years ago. I was in Florence, and he stopped off on his way to Japan."

"I didn't know you went through Florence when you went to Japan."

"You do if you happen to have a daughter living there." She put her elbows on the table, and rested her chin in her hand. "I don't suppose you even knew Ben had a daughter."

"Yes, of course I did."

"Well, I didn't know about you. I mean, I didn't know Marcus had a partner. He was still on his own when Ben went to Texas and I was bundled off to Switzerland."

"It was about that time that I joined Bernstein's."

"I . . . I never knew anyone who looked less like an art dealer. Than you, I mean."

"Perhaps that's just because I'm not an art dealer."

"But . . . you just sold that man Ben's painting."

"No," he corrected her. "I simply accepted the cheque. Marcus had already sold it to him a week ago, but even Mr. Cheeke didn't realise that."

"But you must know something about painting."

"Now, I do. One couldn't work with Marcus for all these years and not have some of his boundless knowledge rub off. But I'm basically a business man, and that's why Marcus asked me to join him."

"But Marcus is the most successful business man I know."

"Exactly, and so successful that the whole venture of the Gallery grew too big for him to handle on his own."

24

Emma continued to regard him, a slight frown between her thickly-marked brows.

"Any more questions?"

She was not disconcerted. "Were you always a very close friend of Marcus?"

"What you really mean is, why did he take me into the firm? And the answer is that Marcus is not only my partner, but my brother-in-law as well. He married my older sister."

"You mean Helen Bernstein is your sister?"

"You remember Helen?"

"But of course. And little David. How are they? You'll send them my love, won't you? You know I used to go and stay with them when Ben came up to London and there wasn't anyone to leave me with at Porthkerris. And when I went to Switzerland, it was Marcus and Helen who put me onto the plane, because Ben had already gone to Texas. Will you tell Helen I'm home, and that you gave me lunch?"

"Yes, of course I will."

"Do they still have that little flat in the Brompton Road?"

"No, as a matter of fact, when my father died, they moved in with me. We all live in our old family house, in Kensington."

"You mean you all live together?"

"Together and apart. Marcus and Helen and David live on the first two floors, and my father's old housekeeper lives in the basement, and I roost in the attics."

"Aren't you married?"

Momentarily, he looked put out. "Well, no, I'm not."

"I was sure you'd be married. You have a very married look about you."

"I don't quite know how to take that."

"Oh, it wasn't meant in a derogatory fashion at all. It's really quite a compliment. I only wish Ben had that look

25

about him. It would make life so much easier for all concerned. Especially me."

"Don't you want to go back and live with him?"

"Yes, of course I do, more than anything. But I don't want it to be a failure. I was never very good at coping with Ben, and I don't suppose I'll be any better now."

"Then why are you going?"

"Well . . ." Under Robert Morrow's cool grey regard, it was difficult to be coherent. She picked up a fork and began to make patterns with it on the white damask cloth. "I don't know. You only have one family. If people belong to each other, they should at least be able to live together. I want to have something to remember. When I'm old I want to be able to remember that once, even if it was only for a few weeks on end, my father and I were making some sort of a life together. Does that sound crazy?"

"No, it doesn't sound crazy, but it sounds as if you might be disappointed."

"I learned all about being disappointed when I was a little girl. It's a luxury I can well do without. Besides, I only plan to stay until it becomes painfully obvious that we cannot stand each other's company for another hour."

"Or," said Robert gently, "until he prefers some other person's company."

Emma's head came up, her eyes a sudden furious blaze of blue. She was, in that instant, her father at his most unscrupulous, when there was no retort too cruel or too cutting to be made. But her anger provoked no reaction, and after a cold pause, she looked down again, and continued to draw patterns on the tablecloth, and only said, "All right. Until then."

The small tension was broken by the return of Marcello bringing their sherry and ready to take the order. Emma chose a dozen oysters and fried chicken; Robert, more conservatively, a consommé and a steak. Then, taking advantage of the interruption, he tactfully changed the subject.

"Tell me about Paris. How was it looking?"

"Wet. Wet and cold and sunny all at once. Does that convey anything to you?"

"Everything."

"You know Paris?"

"I go over on business. I was there last month."

"On business?"

"No, on my way back from Austria. I had three weeks' splendid ski-ing."

"Where did you go?"

"Obergurgl."

"So that's why you're so brown. That's one of the reasons you don't look like an art dealer."

"Perhaps, when my tan fades, I shall look more authentic and be able to command higher prices. How long did you spend in Paris?"

"Two years. I shall miss it. It's so beautiful, and doubly so now all the buildings have been cleaned. And somehow, at this time of the year, there's that special feeling in Paris. That the winter's nearly over and the sun's just a day or so away and it's going to be spring again . . ."

And buds unfolding, and the scream of gulls, swooping over the chopped brown waters of the Seine. And barges, strung like necklaces, slipping away beneath the bridges, and the smell of the Metro, and garlic, and Gauloises. And being with Christopher.

All at once it became important to talk about him, to speak his name, to reassure herself of his existence. She said, casually. "You never met Hester, did you? My stepmother? At least for eighteen months she was my stepmother."

"I know about her."

"And about Christopher? Her son? Do you know about

27

Christopher? Because, quite by chance, Christopher and I met up again in Paris. Just two days ago. And he came, this very morning, and saw me off at Le Bourget."

"You mean . . . you just bumped into each other . . . ?"

"Yes, we really did . . . in a grocer's shop. It could only happen in Paris."

"What was he doing there?"

"Oh, filling in time. He'd been to St. Tropez, but he comes back to England in March to join some repertory theatre or other."

"He's an actor?"

"Yes. Didn't I tell you that? There is just one thing . . . I'm not going to say anything to Ben. You see, Ben never liked Christopher, and I don't think Christopher lost any love over him. To be truthful, I expect they were a little jealous of each other. But there were other things as well, and Ben and Hester didn't exactly part company on the best of terms. I don't want to start off by having a row with Ben about Christopher, so I'm not going to say anything. At least not right away."

"I see."

Emma sighed. "You've got a very stuffy expression on your face. You obviously think I'm being underhand."

"I don't think anything of the sort. And when you've finished making patterns on the tablecloth, your oysters have arrived."

By the time they had finished lunch and drunk their coffee, and Robert had paid the bill, it was half-past one. They got up from the table, and said goodbye to Marcello, and collected the big black umbrella and went downstairs. They walked back to Bernstein's, asked the doorman to get Emma a taxi.

"I'd come with you and put you onto the train, but Peggy has to go out and get herself some lunch."

"I'll be all right."

He took her into the office and unlocked the safe.

"Will twenty pounds be enough?"

She had already forgotten her reason for coming to the Gallery in the first place. "What? Oh, yes, of course . . ." She began to feel for her cheque book, but Robert stopped her.

"Don't bother. Your father has a sort of petty cash account with us. He's always running out of small change when he's in London. We'll put your twenty pounds down to that."

"Well, if you're sure . . ."

"Sure I'm sure. And, Emma, there is one other thing. The man who lent you the pound. Somewhere you have his address. If you find it and give it to me now, I'll see he gets the pound back again."

Emma was amused. Searching for the card, finding it at last, entangled with a French bus ticket and a book of matches, she began to laugh, and when Robert asked her what was so funny, she simply said, "How well you know my father!"

3

It stopped raining at tea-time. There was a subtle lifting of the atmosphere, a freshness in the air. An errant shaft of sunlight even found its way into the gallery, and by five-thirty, when Robert locked up his office, and went out to join the rush hour torrent of home-going humanity, he found that a small breeze had got up and blown the clouds away, leaving the city to sparkle beneath a pale, pellucid blue sky.

It was somehow more than he could bear to plunge into the subterranean stuffiness of the tube, so he walked as far as Knightsbridge, and then got on a bus and rode the rest of the way home.

His house, in Milton Gardens, was separated from the busy artery of the Kensington High Street by a maze of small streets and squares, a pleasant neighbourhood of miniature, early-Victorian houses, cream-painted, and with bright front doors and small gardens that in summer bloomed with lilac and magnolia. The streets had wide pavements where nannies pushed prams and small, well-dressed children walked to their expensive schools and the local dogs were rigorously exercised. After this, Milton Gardens came as something of a let down. It was a terrace of large and shabby houses, and Number Twenty-three, which was Robert's—the centre house, and crowned with the main pediment of the terrace —quite often looked the shabbiest. It had a black front door, and two dried-up bay trees in tubs, and a brass letter-box that Helen always meant to polish, but quite often forgot. The household cars were parked at the pavement's edge—a big dark-green Alvis coupé which was Robert's, and a dusty red Mini which was Helen's. Marcus did not own a car because he had never found time to learn how to drive.

Robert went up the steps, feeling in his pocket for his latch key, and let himself in. The hall was large and spacious, a surprisingly wide and shallow staircase curved up to the first floor. Beyond the staircase, the hall continued in a narrow passage, which led to a glassed door, and the garden. This beguiling vista of distant grass and sun-touched chestnut trees gave the immediate impression of being in the country, and was one of the most endearing aspects of the house.

The front door slammed shut behind him. From the kitchen, his sister Helen called his name.

"Robert."

"Hello!"

He chucked his hat onto the hall table, and went in through the door at the right of the hall. In the old days this room, facing out over the street, had been the family dining-room, but when Robert's father had died, and Marcus and Helen and David had moved in, Helen had converted it into a kitchen-dining-room, with a scrubbed country table, and a

31

pine dresser, crammed with patterned china and a counter, like a bar, behind which she could work. There were also a great many plants in pots, straggling geraniums, and herbs, and bowls of bulbs. Bunches of onions and marketing baskets hung from hooks, and there were recipe books, and racks of wooden spoons, and the cheerfulness of bright rugs and cushions.

Helen was behind her counter now, in a blue and white butcher's apron, peeling mushrooms. The air was filled with fragrant smells—of baking and lemons, and warm butter and the lightest suggestion of garlic. She was an exceptional cook.

She said, "Marcus called from Edinburgh. He's coming home to-night. Did you know?"

"What time?"

"There's a plane at a quarter past five. He was going to try and get a seat on that. It gets in to the terminal at half past seven."

Robert pulled a high stool up to the counter, and perched on it, like a man sitting at a bar.

"Does he want to be met at the airport?"

"No, he'll get the bus in. I thought one of us would go and pick him up. Are you in or out for dinner tonight?"

"It smells so good, I think I'm in."

She smiled. Facing each other across the counter, the family resemblance between them was very marked. Helen was a big woman, tall and heavy-boned, but when she smiled her face and her eyes lit up like a girl's. Her hair, like Robert's, was reddish, but softened by streaks of grey, and she wore it drawn tightly back into a knot, to reveal a small and unexpectedly neat pair of ears. She was proud of her pretty ears, and always wore earrings. She had a whole boxful of them in her dressing-table drawer, and if you didn't know what to give her for a present, you simply bought a pair of earrings. This evening they were green, some sort of semi-precious stone, set in a narrow rope of woven gold, and their colour brought out the green lights in her indeterminate, speckled eyes.

She was forty-two, six years older than Robert, and she had been married to Marcus Bernstein for ten years. Before that she had worked for him, as secretary, receptionist, book-keeper, and on occasions when finances were shaky— as office cleaner as well, and it was as much due to her efforts and faith in Marcus that the Gallery had not merely survived the initial lean patches, but had grown to achieve its present international reputation.

Robert said, "Did Marcus tell you anything . . . about how he got on . . . ?"

"Not much, there wasn't time. But the old Lord of the Glens, whoever he is, has three Raeburns, a Constable and a Turner. So that should give you all something to think about."

"Does he want to sell them?"

"Apparently. He says that at the current price of whisky, he can no longer afford to keep them hanging on the wall. Anyway, we'll hear all about it when Marcus gets back. How about you . . . what have you been doing to-day . . . ?"

"Nothing much. An American called Lowell Cheeke came in and wrote a cheque for a Ben Litton . . ."

"That's fine . . ."

"And . . ." he watched his sister's face . . . "Emma Litton's home."

Helen had started to slice the mushrooms. Now, swiftly, she looked up and her hands were still.

"Emma. You mean Ben's Emma?"

"Flew back from Paris to-day. Came into the Gallery to collect enough money to get her back to Porthkerris."

"Did Marcus know she was coming back?"

"No, I don't think so. I don't think she wrote to anyone except her father."

"And of course Ben wouldn't say a word." Helen made an exasperated face. "Sometimes I could just strangle that man."

Robert was amused. "What would you have done if you'd known she was coming?"

"Well, met her at the airport. Given her lunch. Anything."

"If it's any comfort to you, I gave her lunch."

"Well, good for you." She sliced another mushroom, considering this. "What does she look like now?"

"Attractive, in a rather unusual way."

"Unusual," Helen repeated dryly. "Tell me she's unusual and you tell me nothing I don't already know."

Robert picked up a slice of raw mushroom and ate it, experimentally. "Do you know about her mother?"

"Of course I do." Helen rescued her mushrooms, whisking them out of his reach, and taking them to her cooker, where a pan simmered with warm butter. With another deft movement, she spilled the mushrooms into the butter, and there were faint sizzling sounds and a delicious smell. She stood there, moving the mushrooms around with a wooden spatula, her strong features profiled.

"Who was she?"

"Oh, a little art student, half Ben's age. She was very pretty."

"Was he married to her?"

"Yes, he did marry her. I think, in his way, he was very fond of her. But she was simply a child."

"Did she leave him?"

"No, she died, having Emma."

34

"And then, later on, he married someone called Hester."

Helen turned to look at him, her eyes narrowed. "How do you know about that?"

"Emma told me to-day at lunch."

"Well, I never did! Yes, Hester Ferris. That was years ago."

"But there was a boy. A son. Called Christopher?"

"Don't say he's turned up again."

"Why do you sound so alarmed?"

"You'd sound alarmed, too, if you'd lived through those eighteen months when Ben Litton was married to Hester . . ."

"Tell me."

"Oh, they were murder. For Marcus, for Ben . . . I suppose for Hester, and certainly for me. If Marcus wasn't being roped in to referee some sordid domestic fracas, then he was being showered with ridiculous little bills which Hester said Ben refused to pay. And then, you know how Ben has this phobia about telephones, and Hester put one into her house and Ben tore it out by the roots. And then Ben ran into some sort of mental block and couldn't do any work, and spent all his time in the local pub, and Hester would get hold of Marcus and say that Marcus must come because he was the only person who could do anything with him, and so on, and so on. Marcus aged, visibly, before my eyes. Can you believe that?"

"Yes. But I don't see what it has to do with the boy."

"The boy was one of the bones of contention. Ben couldn't bear him."

"Emma said he was jealous."

"She said that? She was always a perceptive child. I suppose in a way Ben was jealous of Christopher, but Christopher was a devil. He looked like a saint, but his mother spoiled him rotten." She drew her pan of mushrooms away from the heat, and came back to lean her elbows on the counter. "What did Emma say about Christopher?"

"Just that they'd met in Paris."

"What was he doing there?"

"I don't know. I suppose having a holiday. He's an actor. Did you know that?"

"No, but I can well believe it. Was she looking very starry-eyed about him?"

"I should say so, yes. Unless it was the thought of going back to live with her father."

"That's the last thing in the world for her to be starry-eyed about."

"I know that. But when I started to say as much, I near as dammit got my head bitten off."

"Yes, you would. They're as loyal as thieves to each other." She patted his hand. "Don't get involved, Robert; I couldn't bear the strain."

"I'm not involved, simply intrigued."

"Well, for your own peace of mind, take my advice and keep it that way. And while we're on the subject of involvements, Jane Marshall called at lunchtime, and she wants you to ring her up."

"What about, do you know?"

"She didn't say. Just said she'd be in any time after six o'clock. You won't forget, will you?"

"No, I won't forget. But don't you forget, either, that Jane is not an involvement."

"What you're jibbing at, I cannot imagine," said Helen, who had never, with her brother at any rate, bothered to mince words. "She is charming, attractive and efficient."

Robert made no comment on this, and exasperated by his silence, she went on, justifying herself. "You have everything in common, interests, friends, a way of life. Besides, a man of your age should be married. There's nothing so pathetic as an elderly bachelor."

She stopped. There was a pause. Robert said politely, "Have you finished?"

Helen sighed deeply. It was hopeless. She knew, had always known, that no words would provoke Robert into any action that he did not choose to make. He had never been talked into anything in his life. Her outburst had been a waste of breath and she already regretted it.

"Yes, of course I've finished. And I apologise. It's none of my business and I have no right to interfere. It's just that I like Jane, and I want you to be happy. I don't know, Robert. I can't work out what it is you're looking for."

"I don't know either," said Robert. He smiled at his sister, and ran a hand over his head and down the back of his neck, a familiar gesture made when he was either confused or tired. "But I think it has something to do with what exists between you and Marcus."

"Well, I just hope you find it before you drop dead of old age."

He left her to her cooking, collected his hat and the evening paper and a handful of letters, and went upstairs to his own flat. His sitting-room, which looked out over the big garden and the chestnut tree had once been the nursery. It was low-ceilinged, close-carpeted, lined with books, and furnished with as much of his father's stuff as he had been able to get up the staircase. He dropped his hat and the paper and the letters on a chair, and went to the antique bombé cupboard where he kept his drink, and poured himself a whisky and soda. Then he took a cigarette from the box on the coffee table, lit it, and, cradling his glass, went to sit at the desk, to lift the telephone receiver and dial Jane Marshall's number.

She took some time to answer. While he waited, he

doodled on the blotting paper with a pencil, and glanced at his watch and decided that he would have a bath, and change before he went to pick Marcus up at the Cromwell Road terminal. And, as a peace offering to Helen, he would take a bottle of wine downstairs and they would have it with their dinner, the three of them, sitting round the scrubbed table in Helen's kitchen and, inevitably, talking shop. He discovered that he was very tired, and the prospect of such an evening was comforting.

The double burr stopped. A cold voice said, "Jane Marshall here."

She always answered the telephone in this manner, and Robert still found it chilling, although he knew the reason for it. At twenty-six, Jane, with a broken marriage and a divorce behind her, had been forced to start earning her own living, and had ended up with a modest interior decorating business which she ran from her own house. Thus, a single telephone number had to do double duty, and she had long since decided it was prudent to treat an incoming call as potential business until it proved to be otherwise. She had explained this to Robert when he complained about her frigid manner.

"You don't understand. It might be a client ringing up. What's he going to think if I sound all sexy and treacle-voiced?"

"You don't need to sound sexy. Just friendly and pleasant. Why don't you try it? You'd be ripping out walls and running up curtains and loose covers before you knew where you were."

"That's what you think. More likely to be fending him off with a curved upholstery needle."

Now he said, "Jane . . . ?"

"Oh, Robert." Her voice was at once its normal self,

warm and obviously pleased to hear him. "I am sorry, did Helen give you my message?"

"She asked me to call you."

"It's just that I wondered . . . Look, I've been given two tickets for the ballet on Friday. It's La Fille Mal Gardée and I thought you might like to come. Unless you're going away or something."

He looked down at his own hand, drawing boxes, in perfect perspective, on the blotting pad. He heard Helen's voice. *You have everything in common. Interests, friends, a way of life.*

"Robert?"

"Yes. Sorry. No, I'm not going away, and I'd love to come."

"Shall we eat here first?"

"No, we'll go out. I'll book a table."

"I'm glad you can make it." He could tell that she was smiling. "Is Marcus back yet?"

"No, I'm just going to meet him."

"Send him and Helen my love."

"I will."

"See you Friday, then. Goodbye."

"Goodbye, Jane."

After he had replaced the receiver, he did not get up from his desk, but sat there, his chin in his hand, putting the final touches to the last box. When it was finished, he laid down the pencil and reached for his drink, and sat, looking at what he had drawn, and wondered why it should make him think of a long line of suitcases.

Marcus Bernstein came through the glass doors of the terminal building looking, as he always looked, like a refugee or a street musician. His overcoat sagged, his old-fashioned black hat had somehow got turned up in the front, his long, lined face was sallow with tiredness. He carried his bulging brief-case, but his grip had travelled from the airport in the luggage compartment of the bus, and when Robert found him, he was standing, patiently, by the circular conveyor-belt, awaiting its arrival.

He managed to look both humble and dejected, and the casual passer-by would have found it hard to believe that this modest and unassuming man was, in fact, a powerful influence in the art world on both sides of the Atlantic. An Austrian, he had left his native Vienna in 1937, and after the horrors of an alien's war, had burst upon the post-war art world like a bright flame. His obvious knowledge and per-ception quickly drew attention, and his backing of young artists showed an example which other dealers were quick to follow. But his real impact upon the lay public was made in 1949, when he opened his own gallery in Kent Street with an exhibition of abstracts by Ben Litton. Ben, already famous for his pre-war landscapes and portraits, had been moving for some time towards this new medium, and the 1949 exhi-bition was the beginning of a working friendship which rode all personal storms and quarrels. It also marked the end of Marcus' initial struggles, and the start of a long, slow haul to success.

"Marcus!"

He gave a small start, and turned and saw Robert com-ing towards him, and looked surprised, as though he had not expected to be met.

"Hello, Robert. This is very kind of you."

After thirty years in England, his accent was still strongly marked, but Robert no longer noticed it.

"I would have come to the airport, but we weren't sure if you'd get on the plane. Did you have a good flight?"

"It was snowing in Edinburgh."

"It's been raining here all day. Look, there's your bag."

He whipped it off the conveyor-belt . . . "Come on, now . . ."

In the car, waiting for the lights in the Cromwell Road to change, he told Marcus about Mr. Lowell Cheeke returning to Bernstein's to buy the Litton of the deer. Marcus acknowledged this with a grunt, giving the impression that he had known all along that the sale was simply a matter of time. The lights went from red to yellow to green and the car moved forward and Robert said, "And Emma Litton is home from Paris. She flew in this morning. Didn't have any sterling, so she came to the gallery to get you to cash her a cheque. I gave her lunch and twenty pounds and sent her on her way."

"On her way to where?"

"Porthkerris, and Ben."

"I suppose he is there."

"She seemed to think he would be. For the time being, at any rate."

"Poor child," said Marcus.

Robert made no answer to this, and they drove home in silence, each busy with his own thoughts. Back at Milton Gardens, Marcus got out of the car, and went up the steps, feeling for his latchkey, but before he could run it to earth, the door was opened by Helen, and Marcus, in his sagging coat and comic's hat, was silhouetted against the hall light.

She said, "Well, how lovely!" and because he was so much smaller than she, stooped to embrace him, and Robert, extracting Marcus' grip from the boot of the Alvis, tried to work out why it was that they never looked ridiculous.

It seemed to have been dark for a long time. But when the London express came to the junction where she had to change for Porthkerris, and Emma got out of the train, she found that it was not really dark at all. The sky was bright

41

with stars, and the night blown through with a buffeting wind that smelt of the sea. When she had unloaded all her luggage, she stood waiting on the platform for the express to pull out, and above her the tattered leaves of a palm tree rattled incongruously in this restless wind.

The train moved on, and she saw the single porter on the opposite platform, occupied, in a leisurely fashion, with a barrow-load of parcels. When at last he noticed her, he set down the handles of his barrow, and called, across the lines, "Want some help, do you?"

"Yes please."

He jumped down on to the tracks and walked across to her side, and somehow gathered all her belongings into his two arms, and then Emma followed him back across the tracks, and he gave her a hand up on to the other platform.

"Where are you going?"

"Porthkerris."

"Taking the train?"

"Yes."

The smaller train waited on the single line branch track that ran round the coast to Porthkerris. Emma appeared to be the only passenger. She thanked the porter and tipped him and collapsed into a seat. Exhaustion consumed her. Never had a day seemed so long. After a little she was joined by a country woman in a brown hat like a pot. Perhaps she had been shopping, for she carried a bulging, checked leather bag. Minutes passed, the only sound the wind thudding at the closed windows of the train. At last, the engine gave a single whistle and they were off.

It was impossible not to feel excited as familiar landmarks loomed up through the darkness, and were recognised, and then fled past. There were only two small halts before Porthkerris and then, at last, the steep cutting which in spring was quilted in primroses, and then the tunnel, and then the sea was below them, dark as ink, the tide out, the wet sands like satin. Porthkerris was a nest of lights, the curve of the harbour seemed strung with a necklace, and the riding lights of fishing boats were reflected in a maze of shimmering black and gold water.

They had begun to lose speed. The platform slid alongside. The name PORTHKERRIS passed and fell behind. They finally stopped alongside a shiny tin advertisement for boot polish which had been there ever since Emma could remember. Her companion, who had spoken not a word the entire journey, now stood up, opened the door, and stepped sedately out, disappearing into the night. Emma stood in the open door, looking for a porter, but the only visible official was up at the other end of the train, unnecessarily shouting, "Porthkerris! Porthkerris!" She saw him stop to chat to the driver, pushing his cap back off his forehead, and standing with his hands on his hips.

There was an empty barrow by the boot polish advertisement, so she loaded her luggage on to this, and then abandoned it, carrying only a small overnight bag. She began to walk up the platform. In the stationmaster's office, the lights were on, they shone out in warm yellow patches, and a man sat on a bench, reading a newspaper. Emma walked by him, her footsteps ringing on the stone flags, but as she passed, he put down the newspaper and said her name.

Emma stopped, and slowly turned. He folded the newspaper and stood up, and the light seemed to turn his white hair into a halo.

"I thought you were never going to arrive."

"Hello, Ben," said Emma.

"Is the train late, or did I get the times all wrong?"

"I don't think we're late. Perhaps we were late starting from the junction. We seemed to wait there a long time. How did you know what train I'd be on?"

43

"I had a telegram from Bernstein's." *Robert Morrow,* thought Emma. *How kind.* Ben glanced at her bag. "You haven't much luggage."

"I have a barrow-load at the other end of the platform."

He turned to vaguely peer in the direction that Emma indicated. "Never mind. We'll fetch it some other time. Come on, let's get back."

"But someone might take it," Emma protested. "Or it might rain. We'd better tell the porter."

The porter had by now finished his social chat with the engine driver. Ben attracted his attention, told him about Emma's luggage. "Put it somewhere, would you, we'll collect it to-morrow." He gave him five shillings. The porter said, "Yes, Mr. Litton, don't worry, I'll do that," and went off down the platform whistling, tucking the money in the pocket of his waistcoat.

"Well," said Ben again, "what are we waiting for? Come on, let's get moving."

There was no suggestion of a car or a taxi, they were simply going to walk home. They did this by way of a series of narrow short-cuts, steep flight of stone steps, tiny sloping alleys, always leading downhill, until finally they emerged on to the brightly lighted harbour road.

Emma, trudging beside her father, still carrying the overnight bag which he had not thought to carry for her, took a long sideways look at Ben. It was the first time she had seen him for nearly two years, and she thought that no man changed as little as he. He was no fatter, no thinner. His hair, which had been snow-white as long as Emma could remember, was neither thinning nor receding. His face, weathered by years of working in the sun, in the outdoors, by the sea, was darkly tanned and netted with fine lines which could never be described as anything so prosaic as wrinkles. From him, Emma had inherited her strong cheek-bones, and her square chin, but her pale eyes must have come from her mother, for Ben's were deepest beneath craggy brows, and of so dark a brown that in certain lights they looked black.

Even his clothes did not seem to have changed. The sagging corduroy jacket, the narrowly cut trousers, the suède shoes of immense elegance and age—they could have belonged to no one else. To-night his shirt was a faded orange wool, a Paisley cotton handkerchief did duty as a necktie. He had never owned a waistcoat.

They came to his pub, the Sliding Tackle, and Emma half expected him to suggest that they should go in for a drink. She did not want a drink, but she was ravenously hungry. She wondered if there was any food in the cottage. She wondered, in fact, if they were actually going to the cottage. It was quite within the bounds of possibility that Ben had been living in his studio, and would expect Emma to shake down there with him.

She said, tentatively, "I don't even know where we're heading for."

"The cottage, of course. Where did you imagine?"

"I didn't know." They were safely past the pub. "I thought perhaps you might have been living at the studio."

"No, I've been staying at the Sliding Tackle. This is the first time I've been to the cottage."

"Oh," said Emma, glumly.

He caught the inflexion in her voice and reassured her. "It's all right. When they knew at the Sliding Tackle that you were turning up there was a positive deputation of eager ladies all wanting to get the place ready for you. In the end Daniel's wife saw to it for me." Daniel was the barman. "She seemed to think that after all these years everything would be covered in blue mould, like Gorgonzola cheese."

"And was it?"

"No, of course it wasn't. A bit cobwebby, perhaps, but perfectly habitable."

"That was kind of her . . . I must thank her."

"Yes, she'd like that."

The cobbled road climbed steeply away from the harbour. Emma's tired legs ached. Suddenly, and with no word of explanation, Ben removed her bag from her grasp.

"What the hell have you got in this?"

"A toothbrush."

"It weighs like pig-iron. When did you leave Paris, Emma?"

"This morning." It seemed a lifetime ago.

"And how did Bernstein's know about you?"

"I had to go there to get some money. Some sterling. I was given twenty pounds out of your petty cash account. I hope you don't mind."

"I don't give a damn."

They passed his studio, shuttered and dark. "Have you started painting yet?" asked Emma.

"Of course I have. That's what I came back for."

"And the work you did in Japan?"

"I left it in America for the exhibition."

Now, the air was full of the sound of surf, of breakers rolling up on to the beach. The big beach. Their beach. And then the uneven roof of their cottage came into view, illuminated by the street lamp which stood by the blue gate. As they approached it, Ben felt in his jacket pocket for the key, and he went ahead of Emma, through the gate and down the steps, unlocking the door, and letting himself in, switching on the lights as he went, so that in a moment every window was blazing.

Emma followed more slowly. She saw at once the bright flicker of firelight and the almost inhuman cleanliness and order which Daniel's wife had somehow created out of

46

neglect. Everything shone, was scrubbed and whitewashed and polished to within an inch of its life. Cushions had been plumped and placed with geometrical precision. There were no flowers, but the house was pervaded with a strong smell of carbolic.

Ben sniffed and made a face. "Like a bloody hospital," he said. He had put down Emma's bag, and now disappeared in the direction of the kitchen. Emma crossed the room and stood at the fireplace, warming her hands at the blaze. Cautiously, she was beginning to feel more hopeful. She had been afraid that there would be no welcome. But Ben had met her train and there was a fire in the fireplace. No human being could ask for much more.

Over the mantelshelf was the room's only picture, the painting that Ben had done of Emma when she was six years old. It was the first time in her life—and, it transpired, the last—that she had been the centre of his attention, and, for this reason alone she had borne uncomplaining the long hours of sitting, the boredom, the cramps, and his unleashed fury if she moved. For the picture, she had worn a wreath of marguerite daisies, and each day had brought the recurring pleasure of watching Ben's clever hands make a fresh wreath, and then the pride of having him place it on her head, solemnly, as though he were crowning a queen.

He came back into the room. "She's a good woman, that wife of Daniel's. I shall tell him so. I told her to stock up with a few supplies." Emma turned, and saw that he had found himself a bottle of Haigs and a tumbler. "Get me a jug of water, would you, Emma?" A thought occurred to him. "And I suppose another glass, if you want a drink."

"I don't want a drink. But I'm hungry."

"I don't know if she laid in *those* sort of supplies."

"I'll look."

The kitchen, too, had been scoured and scrubbed and

swept. She opened the fridge and found eggs and bacon and a bottle of milk, and there was bread in the bin. She took a jug off a hook on the dresser and filled it with cold water, and carried it back into the sitting-room. Ben was wandering about, fiddling with the lamps, trying to find something wrong. He had always hated this house.

She said, "Do you want me to cook you some scrambled eggs?"

"What? Oh, no, I don't want anything. You know, it's odd being back here. I keep feeling Hester's going to appear and tell us to start doing something we don't want to."

Emma thought of Christopher. She said, "Oh, poor Hester."

"Poor nothing. Interfering bitch."

She went back to the kitchen, found a saucepan, a bowl, some butter. From the living-room, she could hear the continued sounds of Ben's restlessness. He opened and shut doors, drew a curtain, kicked a log back on to the fire. Presently, he appeared in the kitchen doorway, a cigarette in one hand, his glass cradled in the other. He watched Emma, stirring eggs. He said, "You've grown up, haven't you?"

"I'm nineteen. Whether I've grown up or not, I really wouldn't know."

"It's odd, your not being a little girl any longer."

"You'll get used to it."

"Yes, I suppose so. How long are you going to stay?"

"Let's say I've made no plans for going away again."

"You mean, you want to live here?"

"For the time being."

"With me?"

Emma glanced at him, over her shoulder. "Would that be so painful?"

"I don't know," said Ben. "I've never tried it."

"That's why I came back. I thought perhaps it was time you did."

"You couldn't, by any chance, be reproaching me?"

"Why should I reproach you?"

"Because I abandoned you, and went off to teach in Texas. Because I never came to see you in Switzerland. Because I wouldn't let you come to Japan."

"If I really minded about those things, I shouldn't have wanted to come back."

"And supposing I decide to go away again?"

"Are you going to go?"

"No." He looked down at his drink. "Not for the moment. At the moment I'm tired. I've come back for a bit of peace." He looked up again. "But I shan't stay here for ever."

"I shan't stay here for ever, either," said Emma. She put the toast on a plate, the egg on the toast, opened a drawer to find a knife and fork.

Ben watched all this with some agitation. "You aren't going to be an efficient little housewife, are you? Another Hester? If so, I shall throw you out."

"I couldn't be efficient if I tried. If it's any comfort to you, I miss trains, burn food, lose money, drop things. I had a sun hat, this morning, in Paris, but by the time I'd got to Porthkerris, it had gone. How could anyone lose a sun hat in this country, in February?"

But he was still not convinced. "Won't you want to be driving around in a car all the time?"

"I don't know how to drive a car."

"And television and telephones and all that rubbish?"

"They've never figured largely in my life."

He laughed then, and Emma wondered if there was something wrong in thinking your own father so attractive.

He said, "You know, I wasn't sure how well this was

49

going to work. But under such favourable circumstances, I can only say I'm glad you came back. Welcome home."

And he raised his glass to Emma and finished his drink, and then went back to the sitting-room to retrieve the bottle and pour himself the other half.

4

The bar of the Sliding Tackle was small and snug, blackly panelled, very old. It boasted only one tiny window, which looked out over the harbour, so that a visitor's first impression, as he came in from the glaring outside light, was one of utter darkness. Later, when his eyes became accustomed to the gloom, other peculiarities became evident, the most prominent being that there were not two parallel lines in the place, for over the centuries the little pub had settled into its foundations, like a deep sleeper in a comfortable bed, and various irregularities, like optical illusions, were apt to make potential customers feel intoxicated before they had even downed their first drink. The flagged floor sank in one direction, displaying a sinister gap between stone and wainscoting. The blackened beam, which formed the framework of the bar itself, sloped in another. And the white-washed

ceiling had such a lethal tilt to it that the landlord had been
driven to put up notices saying "Watch That Beam" and
"Mind Your Head."

Over the years the Sliding Tackle had remained, stubbornly, itself. Set in the old and unfashionable part of
Porthkerris, slap on the harbour, with no space for chi-chi
terraces or tea gardens, it had managed to resist the spate of
summer tourism which engulfed the rest of the town. It had
its regulars, who came to drink, and talk in comfortable,
undemanding grunts, and play shove-ha'penny. It had a dart
board and a small blackened grate where, winter and summer, a fire always burned. It had Daniel, the barman, and
Fred, turnip-faced and squint-eyed, who was employed in
the summer cleaning trash from the beaches and hiring out
deck chairs, and spent the rest of the year blissfully drinking
his takings.

And it had Ben Litton.

"It's a matter of priorities," said Marcus, as he and Robert set forth in the Alvis to run Ben Litton to earth. It was so
fine that Robert had put the hood down, and so Marcus
wore, with his habitual black overcoat, a tweed cap like a
mushroom that looked as though it had been bought for
some other person. "Priorities and timing. At mid-day on a
Sunday, the first place to look is the Sliding Tackle. And if he
isn't there, which I very much doubt, we'll go on to the
studio, then he'll be at the cottage."

"Or maybe, on such a wonderful morning, just out and
about?"

"I don't think so. This is his drinking time, and as far as
that is concerned, he has always been a creature of habit."

Still only March, it was indeed a freak day of unbelievable beauty. The sky was cloudless. The sea, driven
obliquely into the curve of the bay by a buffeting north-west

wind, lay streaked before them in every shade of blue,
from deep indigo to palest turquoise. From the top of the
hill, the view stretched to infinity, distant headlands merging
into a haze that suggested the full heat of midsummer. And
below, down the twisting road, the town dropped steeply, a
jumble of narrow cobbled lanes, and white-washed houses,
and bleached, crooked roofs, clustered around the harbour.

Each year, during the three months of summer,
Porthkerris became a small hell on earth. Its inadequate
streets were jammed with cars, its pavement overflowed
with underdressed humanity, its shops spilled over with
postcards, sun hats, sand-shoes, shrimping-nets, surfboards
and inflatable plastic cushions. On the big beach the tents
and the bathing huts went up, and the cafés opened, their
terraces crammed with round iron tables, speared by umbrellas. Orange banners flapped in the wind, advertising
Raspberry Sticks, and Frozen Chocolate-Coated Clusters
and other horrors, and if these were not sustenance enough,
there were Cornish Splits for sale, and pasties, filled with
soggy grey potato.

And around Whitsun, the amusement arcade opened
up, with pin-ball machines and juke boxes blaring, and perhaps another cluster of ramshackle but picturesque houses
would go down before the bulldozers, to clear the space for
yet another car park, and the residents, and the people who
loved the town, and the artists, would be horrified witnesses
to this rape and say, *It's worse than ever. It is ruined. We can
stay no longer.* But each autumn, once the last train had
borne away the last peeling-nosed invader, Porthkerris settled back, miraculously, in its normal tempo. The shops put
up their shutters. The tents came down, and the beaches
were washed clean by the winter storms. The only flags
which flew were lines of washing, flapping from house to

house, like pastel-coloured bunting, or propped high over the greenswards where the fishermen spread their nets to dry.

And it was then that the old magic reasserted itself, and it became easy to understand why a man like Ben Litton should return time and time again, like a homing pigeon, for refreshment, and the security of familiar things, to be caught up once more in the painter's obsession with colour and light.

The Sliding Tackle was at the far end of the harbour road. Robert drew up outside its crooked porch and killed the engine. It was very warm and quiet. The tide was out, the harbour full of clean sand and seaweed and screaming gulls. Some children, coaxed out by the sunshine, played with buckets and spades, watched over by a couple of knitting grannies in pinafores and hairnets, and a scrawny black cat sat on the cobbles and washed its ears.

Marcus got out of the car. "I'll go and see if he's inside. You wait here."

Robert took a cigarette from the packet on the dashboard and lit it, and watched the cat. Above his head the inn sign creaked in the wind, and a gull came and sat on it and eyed Robert with malevolence, screaming defiance. Two men came down the road, walking with the slow righteous gait of a restful Methodist Sunday. They wore navy blue guernseys and white cloth caps.

" 'Morning," they said as they passed.

"Lovely day," said Robert.

"Yes. Lovely."

After a little, Marcus appeared once more. "All right, I've found him."

"What about Emma?"

"He says she's back at the studio. Whitewashing."

"Want me to go and get her?"

"If you would. It's . . ." he glanced at his watch, "twelve-fifteen. Suppose you're back here at one. I said we'd lunch at one-thirty."

"Right. I'll walk. It's not worth taking the car."

"Can you remember the way?"

"Of course." He had been before, twice, to Porthkerris, chasing up Ben Litton for some reason or other when Marcus had not been available to do it for himself. Ben's phobia about telephones and cars and all forms of communication, presented, from time to time, the most hideous complications, and Marcus had long since accepted the fact that it was quicker to make the journey from London to Cornwall and beard the lion in his den than to wait for an answer to the most impassioned of reply-paid telegrams.

He got out of the car and slammed the door shut. "Do you want me to tell her what it's all about, or shall I leave that pleasant task to you?"

Marcus grinned. "You tell her."

Robert pulled off his narrow tweed cap and dropped it on to the driving seat. He said, amiably, "You bastard."

He had had a letter from Emma, a week or two after she passed through London.

DearRobert,

If I call Marcus Marcus, I can't possibly call you Mr. Morrow, can I? No, of course I can't, not possibly. I should have written at once to thank you so very much for the lunch and for letting me have the money, and for letting Ben know that I was on the train. He actually came to meet me at the station. Everything is going wonderfully well, so far we haven't had a row, and Ben is working like a fiend on four canvases at once.

I didn't lose any of my luggage except the sun hat, which I'm sure someone stole.

My love to Marcus. And you.

Emma.

Now, he made his way through the baffling maze of narrow streets and tightly-packed houses that led to the north shore of the town. Here, there was another beach, a bleak and unprotected bay only esteemed for the long surfing rollers which poured in, straight from the Atlantic. Ben Litton's studio faced out over this beach. Once, long ago, it had been a net store and its only access was a cobbled ramp which sloped down from the street to a double, black-tarred door. There was a printed sign with his name, and an immense iron knocker, and Robert took hold of this and banged it, and called "Emma."

There was no reply. He opened the door, and it was immediately almost torn from his hand by a gust of wind which poured, like a torrent of water, through the open window on the far side of the studio. Once the door had slammed shut again behind him, the draught subsided. The studio was empty and bitterly cold. There was no sign of Emma, but a step ladder and white-wash brush and bucket bore witness to her recent occupation. She had finished the whole of one wall, but when he went to touch it with his hand, he found that it was still cold and damp.

From the middle of this wall protruded an ugly old-fashioned stove, empty now and unlit, and beside it a gas ring, a battered kettle, and an upturned orange box containing blue and white striped mugs and a jar of sugar lumps. On the opposite side of the room stood Ben's work table, littered with drawings and papers, tubes of paint, and hundreds of pencils and brushes all contained on sheets of corrugated cardboard. The wall above this table was dark and dirty with age, and smeared with the scrapings of countless palette knives, that had built up, over the years, into a crustaceous shell of colour. At the top of the desk was a narrow level shelf, and on this ranged a selection of *objets trouvés* which at some time or another had caught Ben's eye. A stone from the shore, a fossilized starfish. A blue jug of dried grasses. A postcard reproduction of a Picasso; a piece of bleached driftwood, carved by sea and wind to abstract sculpture. There were photographs, a fan of curling snapshots, arranged in an old silver menu-holder; an invitation to a private view that had taken place six years ago, and, finally, a heavy, old-fashioned pair of binoculars.

At floor level, the walls were stacked with leaning canvases, and in the middle of the room the current work stood, easeled and shrouded with a faded pink cloth. Turned towards the empty stove was a sagging sofa, draped in what looked like the remains of an Arabic rug. There was also an old kitchen table, with its legs cut short, and on this a tin of cigarettes, and an overflowing ashtray, a pile of "Studios," and a green glass bowl, full of painted china eggs.

The north wall was all glass, squared off by narrow wooden partitions and designed so that its lower portions would slide aside. Along the foot of this was a long seat, piled with cushions, and from beneath this protruded further ill-assorted flotsam. The spars of a boat, a stack of surf boards, and a crate of empty bottles, and, in the middle, beneath the open window, two iron hooks had been screwed into the floor, and on to those were looped the spliced ends of a rope ladder. This disappeared out of the window, and Robert, going to investigate, saw that it dropped straight down to the sand, twenty feet below.

The beach appeared to be empty. The ebb tide had left it a sweep of hard clean sand, divided from the sky by a narrow line of frothing white breakers. Further inshore, there was a stratum of rock, crusted with shellfish and sea-weed, and over this the seagulls hovered, occasionally pouncing to fight and scream over some prize. Robert sat on the windowseat, and lit himself a cigarette. When he looked up again, a figure had appeared on the horizon, right on the edge of the sea. It wore a long white gown, like an Arab's, and as it walked back towards the studio, appeared to be wrestling with some large and unidentifiable red package.

He remembered the binoculars on Ben's table and went to fetch them. Focused, the figure sprang into relief, and revealed itself as Emma Litton, long hair blowing, dressed in a huge white towelling robe and lugging, with some difficulty, for the wind kept catching it broadside and jerking it out of her grasp, a scarlet surfboard.

"You surely haven't been swimming?"

Emma, struggling with the surfboard, had not seen him at the window. Now, with a hand on the rope ladder, she nearly jumped out of her skin at the sound of his voice. She looked up, trailing the surfboard in the sand, her wet black hair ripped to ribbons by the wind.

"Yes, I have, and what a fright you gave me. How long have you been there?"

"About ten minutes. How are you going to get the surf-board up the ladder?"

"I was wondering that, but now you've turned up all my problems are solved. There's a rope under the seat. If you chuck one end down, I'll tie it on, and you can pull it up for me."

This was duly accomplished. Robert hauled the board through the open window, and hard on its heels came Emma herself, her face and hands and feet crusted with dry sand, and her black lashes spiked like starfish.

She knelt on the window seat, and laughed at him.

"Now, wasn't that the luckiest thing! What would I have done? I could hardly get it over the beach, let alone up the ladder."

Beneath the sand, her face looked blue with cold. He said, "Come along in, and get the window shut . . . that wind's freezing. How could you bear to go and swim? You'll die of pneumonia."

"No, I won't." She stepped down onto the floor, and watched him furl the ladder in and slide the window shut. It did not fit properly and there was still a draught like the edge of a knife. "Anyway, I'm used to it. We always used to swim in April when we were children."

"This isn't April. It's March. It's winter. What would your father say?"

"Oh, he wouldn't say anything. And it's such an utterly gorgeous day and I was sick of whitewashing . . . have you seen my lovely clean wall? The only thing is, it makes the rest of the studio look like a slum. Besides, I wasn't swimming, I was surfing, and the breakers kept me warm." And then, without any noticeable change of expression, "Have you come to see Ben? He's down at the Sliding Tackle."

"Yes, I know."

"How do you know?"

"Because I left Marcus there with him."

"Marcus." She raised her strongly-marked eyebrows, considering this. "Has Marcus come too? My goodness, it must be important business!"

She shivered slightly.

Robert said, "Do get some clothes on."

"Oh, I'm all right." She went to take a cigarette from the table, and lit it, and then collapsed on to the old sofa, flat on her back, with her feet propped on the arm.

"Did you get my letter?"

"Yes, I did." With Emma taking up all the sofa, there

was nowhere to sit but on the table, so he eased the pile of magazines on to the floor, and sat there. "I was sorry about your sun hat."

Emma laughed. "But glad about Ben?"

"Of course."

"It's amazing how well it's working. Unbelievable. And he really likes having me around."

"I never imagined for a moment that he wouldn't."

"Oh, don't start being gallant. You know you did. At lunch that day, you were all quizzical eyebrows and scepticism. But you see, it really is the perfect arrangement. Ben doesn't have to pay me to keep house for him, or be bothered with tedious details like days off and insurance stamps, nor does he have to become emotionally involved. He never knew that life could be so simple."

"Have you heard from Christopher?"

Emma turned her head sideways to look at him. "How do you know about Christopher?"

"You told me yourself. At Marcello's. Remember?"

"So I did. No, I haven't heard. But he'll be at Brookford by now, in the thick of rehearsals. He won't have had time to write. Anyway, there's been such a lot to do here, getting the cottage organised and cooking and things. Don't believe people when they say that artists never eat. Ben's inner man is quite insatiable."

"Have you told him you met up with Christopher again?"

"Good heavens, no! And spoil the even tenor of our life? I haven't even mentioned his name. You know, you look much nicer in those tweedy sort of clothes than you do in the London kind. I thought when I first saw you that you weren't the type to spend his days buttoned up in a charcoal grey suit. When did you get down here?"

"We drove yesterday afternoon. We spent last night at the Castle."

Emma made a face. "In with all the potted palms and the cashmere cardigans. Ugh!"

"It's very comfortable."

"The central heating gives me hay fever. I can't even breathe."

She stubbed her half-smoked cigarette out in the overflowing ashtray, and swung her feet off the sofa, and stood up and walked away from him, towards the window, untying the sash of the robe as she went. She took a pile of clothes from beneath a cushion, and with her back to him, started to dress. She said, "Why did you and Marcus come together?"

"Marcus doesn't drive."

"There are trains. And that wasn't what I meant."

"No, I know." He picked up one of the painted china eggs and began to play with it as an Arab handles a string of worry beads. "We've come to try and persuade Ben to go back to the United States."

There was a sudden great squall of wind. It broke over the glass window of the studio like a wave, poured, roaring over the roof above them, with the thunder of a passing train. A cluster of gulls rose screaming from the rocks, were flung across the sky. And then, as suddenly, it was over.

Emma said, "Why does he have to go back?"

"This retrospective exhibition."

She dropped the white towelling robe, and stood silhouetted, in jeans, pulling a navy blue sweater over her head.

"But I thought he and Marcus fixed all that when they were in New York in January."

"We thought so too. But you see, this exhibition is being sponsored by a private individual."

"I know," said Emma, turning, and flipping her dark

61

hair free of the turtle-neck of the sweater. "I read all about it in *Réalités*. Mrs. Kenneth Ryan. The widow of the wealthy man whose memorial is the Queenstown Museum of Fine Arts. You see how well informed I am. I hope you're impressed."

"And Mrs. Kenneth Ryan wants a private view."

"Then why didn't she say so?"

"Because she wasn't in New York. She was sunning it in Nassau or the Bahamas or Palm Beach or somewhere. They never met her. They only saw the curator of the museum."

"And now Mrs. Ryan wants Ben Litton to go back, so that she can throw a nice little champagne party and show him off, like a trophy, to all her influential friends. It makes me sick."

"She's done more than decide, Emma. She's come to persuade him."

"You mean come to England?"

"I mean come to England, come to Bernstein's, come to Porthkerris. She drove down with Marcus and me yesterday and at this very moment, is sitting in the bar of the Castle Hotel, drinking very cold Martinis and waiting for us all to go and have lunch with her."

"Well, I for one am not going."

"You have to. We're all expected." He glanced at his wrist-watch. "And we're running late. Do hurry up."

"Does Ben know about the private view?"

"He will by now. Marcus will have told him."

She picked up a brown sailcloth smock off the floor and pulled it on over her sweater. As her head came through the neck, she said, "Ben may not want to go."

"You mean you don't want him to go?"

"I mean that he's settled down here again. He's not prowling, he's not restless, he's not even drinking very much. He's working like a young man, and what he's doing is fresh and new and better than ever. Ben is sixty, you know. Looking at him, it's hard to believe, but he's nearly sixty. Isn't it possible that all this hopping about all over the world may no longer stimulate him, but simply wear him out?" She came back to the sofa to sit down, facing Robert, her earnest face on a level with his own. "Please. If he doesn't want to go, don't try to persuade him."

Robert still held the china egg. He looked at it intently as though its convolutions of blue and green would miraculously provide the answer to every problem. Then, with care, he laid it back in the glass dish, along with its fellows.

He said, "You talk as though this were something important, as though he were returning to the States to teach again, as though he weren't going to come back for years. But it isn't. It's simply a party. He needn't be away for more than a few days." She opened her mouth with a fresh protest, but he talked her down. "And you mustn't forget that this exhibition is a great tribute to Ben. A lot of money's been ploughed into it, and a great deal of organization, and perhaps the least he can do . . ."

Furiously, Emma interrupted. "The least he can do is go and parade up and down like a pet monkey, for some fat old American. And what makes it so awful is that he likes that sort of thing. That's what I hate, that he likes it."

"So he likes it. So, if he wants to, he'll go."

She was silenced. She sat, eyes downcast, her mouth sulky as a child's. Robert finished his cigarette and stubbed it out, and stood up and said, more gently, "Now, do come on or we're going to be late. Have you got a coat?"

"No."

"Some shoes then, you must have some shoes."

She felt under the sofa and produced a pair of thong sandals, and stood up, thrusting her bare feet into them. Her

63

feet were still covered in sand, and the sail-cloth smock spotted in whitewash.

She said, "I can't go to the Castle, for lunch, looking like this."

"Nonsense." He tried to sound bracing. "You'll give the residents something to talk about. Brighten their dull lives no end."

"Isn't there time to go back to the cottage? I haven't even got a comb."

"There'll be a comb at the hotel."

"But . . ."

"There simply isn't time. We're late already. Now come along . . ."

They went together, out of the studio and up the ramp, and into the sunlit street, and began to walk back towards the harbour. After the chill of the studio the air felt warm, and the brightness of the sea was reflected from the whitewashed walls of houses, and assailed the eye like the glare off snow.

5

Emma did not want to go into the Sliding Tackle.

"I'll wait here. You go and prise them out."

"All right."

He went across the cobbles, and she noticed how he had to duck his tall head to get in under the porch. The door of the pub swung shut behind him. She wandered over to his car and inspected it with interest, because it belonged to him, and should therefore provide further clues to his character, as a shelf of book-titles will do, or the pictures that a man hangs on his walls. But, apart from the fact that it was dark-green, had fog lights and wire wheels and a couple of car-club badges, the Alvis gave little away. Inside on the driving-seat was a tweed cap; cigarettes in the dashboard cupboard, a book of maps. On the back seat, neatly folded, a thick, expensive-looking tartan rug. She decided that he was either trusting, or careless, but also lucky, for the rug had not been stolen.

A gust of wind blew in from the sea and Emma shivered. After the swim and the session in the draughty studio, she still was very cold. Her hands had gone numb, quite colourless, the fingernails tinged with blue. But the metal of the car was warm, and, for comfort, she leaned against it, spreadeagled across the bonnet, with her hands splayed like starfish.

The pub door opened and Robert Morrow emerged once more, ducking cautiously. He was alone.

"Aren't they there?"

"No. We're late, and they got fed up with waiting, so they got a lift back to the hotel." He opened the driving-seat door, picked up his cap and pulled it on, jerked down over his nose, to add yet another sharp angle to his formidable profile. "Come on . . ." And he leaned over and opened the other door, and Emma unpeeled herself from the bonnet, and slid in beside him.

They left the harbour behind and below them, roared up through the town, up the steep narrow streets, up between terraces of prim houses, and the signs which said Bed and Breakfast, and front gardens where sad palm trees tossed their heads in the alien wind. They came out on to the main road, still climbing, turned into the drive of the Castle Hotel; climbed on, between banks of hydrangeas, and landward-leaning elm trees, and at last came out at the very top of the hill, into an open space of tennis courts, and lawns, and a miniature golf course. The hotel had once been a country house, and prided itself on its authentic atmosphere. A white post and chain fence kept cars away from the gravel sweep in front of the hotel, and here, in deck chairs, sat a handful of hardy residents, scarved, gloved and swaddled in rugs, like the passengers of some trans-Atlantic liner. They read books or newspapers, but when the Alvis roared up the drive and drew up with a massive scrunch of gravel, these were lowered, and in some cases, spectacles were removed, and Robert and Emma's progress observed and noted as though they were visitors from another planet.

Robert said, "We're probably the first exciting thing to happen since the manager fell into the swimming-pool."

Once inside the revolving doors, the heat of the place struck like a newly-opened oven. Emma professed to despise such comfort, but to-day it was blissfully welcome.

She said, "I expect they'll be in the bar. You go, I'll be there in a moment. I must try and get rid of some of this sand."

In the Ladies', she washed her hands and her face, and rubbed the sand off her feet on to the back of her jeans, like a schoolboy trying to polish his shoes. There was a pretentious set of brushes and combs on a be-ruffled dressing-table, and she used the comb on the snarls of her hair, breaking half the teeth, but reducing the tangled mass into some sort of order. As she turned back for the door, she caught sight of herself in the long mirror. No make-up, faded jeans, white-wash stains. She pulled off the offending smock, and then was infuriated with herself for minding about anything so trivial as her own personal appearance, and pulled it on again. They would think she was a beatnik art student. A model. Ben Litton's mistress. Let them. As Robert Morrow had so rightly said, it would give them something to talk about.

But as she emerged from the Ladies' and went down the long, carpeted hall, she was grateful to see that Robert Morrow had not abandoned her and gone to join the others, as she had told him to, but was waiting for her by the porter's desk, reading a Sunday paper which had been left on a chair. When he saw her coming, he folded the paper and tossed it down again, and gave her a grin of encouragement.

"You've done splendidly," he said.

"I've ruined the hotel comb. Ever so nice it was, too, one of a matching set. You didn't need to wait. I've been before and I know the way . . ."

"Come along, then."

It was a quarter to two, and the busy Sunday lunchtime session was over. Only a few serious drinkers still sat at the bar, cradling their gin and tonics and beginning to look a bit red in the face. Ben Litton, Marcus Bernstein and Mrs. Kenneth Ryan were over on the other side of the room, grouped in the bay formed by a huge picture window. Mrs. Ryan was on the window-seat, against a back drop like a travel agent's poster—a shout of blue sea, a sweep of sky, and the green undulations of the miniature golf course. The two men, Ben in his French workman's *bleus,* and Marcus in his dark suit, were talking, turned slightly towards her, so that it was Mrs. Ryan who first saw Emma and Robert.

"Well, look who's here . . ." she said.

They turned. Ben remained sitting, but Marcus stood up and came to greet Emma, his arms outstretched, his pleasure at seeing her both genuine and demonstrative and very un-British. He could on occasion be almost embarrassingly Austrian.

"Emma, my darling child. Here you are at last." He put his hands to her shoulders and kissed her, formally, on both cheeks. "What a pleasure to see you again, after this very long time. How long is it? Five years? Six years? What a lot we have to talk about. Come along, and meet Mrs. Ryan." He took her hand to lead her over. ". . . But your hand is like a block of ice. What have you been doing?"

"Nothing," said Emma, catching Robert's eyes, and daring him to say more.

"And your bare feet . . . how can you stand it? Mrs. Ryan, this is Ben's daughter, Emma, but don't shake hands with her, or you will die of shock."

"I can think of worse ways to die," said Mrs. Ryan, and held out her hand. "How do you do?"

They shook hands. "I must say, you are very cold."

On an insane impulse, Emma said, "I was swimming. That's why we're late. And why I'm so untidy. There wasn't time to go back to change."

"Oh, but you don't look untidy, you look charming. Sit down . . . we have time for another drink, don't we? The dining-room isn't going to shut down on us or anything like that. Robert, would you be a darling, and order another round for us. What would you like, Emma?"

"I . . . I don't really want anything." Ben gave a small cough. "Well . . . a glass of sherry."

"And we're all drinking Martinis, Robert. If you want one too?" Emma lowered herself carefully on to the chair that Marcus had vacated, aware of her father watching her from the other side of the table.

"I simply don't believe," said Mrs. Ryan, "that you really have been swimming."

"Not really. I just went in and out again. There were huge waves."

"But won't you get the most terrible chill? It can't be good for you." She turned to Ben. "You don't approve, surely, of swimming when it's as cold as this? Haven't you got any influece on your daughter?"

Her voice was gay and teasing. Ben made some reply, and she went on, telling him that he should be ashamed of himself . . . that she could see he was an outrageous father . . .

Emma did not listen. She was far too busy looking. For Mrs. Ryan was not old and fat, but young and beautiful and very attractive, and from the top of her smoothly-coiffed golden blonde head to the tips of her shining crocodile pumps there was no single detail that did not give active pleasure. Her eyes were enormous and blue as violets, her mouth full and sweet-tempered, and when she smiled, as she did now, revealed two perfect rows of even, white, American teeth. She wore a most becoming suit of rose-pink tweed, the collar and cuffs edged with starched white pique. Diamonds sparkled from her ears, her lapel, her neatly-manicured hands. There was nothing vulgar about her, nothing brash. Even her scent was flower-like.

". . . The fact that she has been away from you for six years is all the more reason for you to take care of her now."

"I don't take care of her . . . she takes care of me . . ."

"Now there is a real man talking . . ." Her soft, southern voice made the words sound like a caress.

Emma's eyes moved round to her father. His attitude was a characteristic one, legs crossed, right elbow resting on his knee, his chin supported by his thumb, a cigarette between his fingers, its smoke rising before his eyes. The eyes were dark as black coffee, deeply shadowed, and they watched Mrs. Ryan as though she were a fascinating new specimen, caught between the glass plates of a laboratory slide.

"Emma, your drink."

It was Marcus. She dragged her eyes from Ben and Mrs. Ryan and turned to him in relief.

"Oh, thank you . . ."

He sat beside her. "Robert has told you about the private view?"

"Yes, he told me."

"Are you angry with us?"

70

"No." And this was true. You could not be angry with such an honest man who came so instantly to the point.

"But you don't want him to go?"

"Did Robert say that?"

"No, he didn't say. But I know you very well. And I know how long you've waited to be with Ben. But it's only for a little while."

"Yes." She looked down at her drink. "He really is going, then?"

"Yes, he really is going. But not until the end of the month."

"I see."

Marcus said, gently, ". . . if you wanted to go with him . . ."

"No. No, I don't want to go to America."

"Do you mind being alone?"

"No. It doesn't bother me. And, as you say, it won't be for long."

"You could come to London, and stay with Helen and myself. You could have David's room."

"Where would David sleep?"

"It is so sad, he is away at boarding school. It broke my heart, but I am now an Englishman and my son was torn from me at eight years old. Come and stay, Emma. In London, there is a lot to see. The Tate Gallery has been re-hung, and it is a masterpiece . . ."

Despite herself Emma began to smile.

"What are you laughing about, you horrible child?"

"I'm laughing at your shamelessness. You take my father away with one hand, and offer me the Tate Gallery with the other. And," she added, dropping her voice, "nobody bothered to tell me that Mrs. Kenneth Ryan was the Beauty Queen of Southern Virginia."

"We didn't know," said Marcus. "We had never seen

71

her. She flew to England on an impulse, she walked into the Bernstein galleries the day before yesterday and said she wanted to see Ben Litton, and that was the first time I had ever set eyes on her."

"Well, she's certainly worth setting eyes on."

"Yes," said Marcus. He looked across at Mrs. Ryan with his sad, hound's eyes. He looked at Ben. He looked back into his Martini, and touched the sliver of lemon peel with his forefinger. "Yes," he said again.

Their arrival, late, in the dining-room caused something of a stir. The best table had been reserved for them, the round one in the window, and it was necessary to cross the length of the floor to get there. Mrs. Ryan led the way, aware of adulation from every eye in the room, and apparently unconcerned. She was quite used to it. Behind her came Marcus, shabby, but oddly distinguished and obviously interesting. Then Robert and Emma, and finally Ben. Ben fell behind to stub out his cigarette and made what amounted to a star entrance, stopping for a moment in the doorway to speak to the head waiter, so that by the time he did move forward into the room, he was the sole centre of attraction.

Ben Litton . . . There's Ben Litton, the whispers went up, as he walked between the tables, magnificent in his blue French overalls, the red and white scarf knotted at his throat, his white hair thick as a young man's, a quiff like a comma falling across his forehead.

Ben Litton . . . you know, the painter.

It was exciting. Everybody knew that Ben Litton had a studio in Porthkerris, but if you were determined to actually see him, you had to make your way down to the town, and find a fisherman's pub called the Sliding Tackle, and there sit, in the stuffy gloom, making a glass of warm beer last as long as possible, and wait for him to come. It was rather like a strange form of bird-watching.

But to-day, Ben Litton had abandoned his usual haunts, and was here, at the Castle Hotel, about to eat Sunday lunch, like any other ordinary human being. The mountain had come to Mahomet. An elderly lady stared openly at him through her lorgnette, and a visiting Texan was heard mourning the fact that he had left his flash camera in the bedroom.

Emma caught Robert Morrow's eye, and just managed to suppress a snort of laughter.

Ben reached the table at last, settled himself in the place of honour at Mrs. Ryan's right, picked up a menu, and suggested, simply by raising a finger, that the wine waiter should be fetched. Gradually, the excitement in the dining-room died down, but it was obvious that for the rest of the meal they would be the object of all attention.

Emma said to Robert, "I know I shouldn't approve—I should be ashamed of such blatant exhibitionism, but somehow, he gets away with it every time."

"Well, at least it's made you laugh, and you've stopped looking all pinched and nervous."

"You might have told me Mrs. Ryan was young and beautiful."

"She's certainly beautiful. But I don't think she's as young as she appears. Well-preserved more like it."

"That's the sort of bitchy remark a woman would make."

"I'm sorry. It was meant with the best will in the world."

"You still should have told me."

"You never asked."

"No, but I made some remark about fat old Americans, and even then you didn't put me right."

"Perhaps I didn't realise that it was so important to you."

"A beautiful woman and Ben Litton, and you didn't realise it was important? It's more than that; it's lethal. One thing, you and Marcus won't have to do any persuading. Ben is going to America. One sweep of those lashes, and he was already mid-Atlantic."

"I don't think you're being entirely fair. The longest lashes in the world wouldn't sweep him into anything he didn't want to do."

"No, but he could never resist a challenge."

Her voice was cold.

Robert said, "Emma."

She turned to look at him. "What?"

"Your resentment is showing." He measured between his forefinger and thumb. "Just the very smallest amount."

"Yes . . . well . . ." She decided to change the subject. "When do you go back to London?"

"This very afternoon." He glanced at his watch. "We're running late, as it is. We'll need to leave, as soon as I can coax Little Miss Millions away."

But Mrs. Ryan was not to be hurried. The luncheon wore on through four courses, through wine and brandy and coffee, served in the now-empty dining-room, because she did not want to move from their table. At last, taking advantage of a pause in the conversation, Robert cleared his throat, and said, "Marcus, I am sorry to interrupt, but I really think we should make a start, we've got a three hundred mile drive."

Mrs. Ryan seemed astonished. "But whatever time is it?"

"Nearly four o'clock."

She laughed. "Already! It's like being in Spain. I once went to a lunch party in Spain, and we didn't get up from the table until half-past seven in the evening. Why does time have to go so fast when you're really enjoying yourself?"

"Cause and effect," said Ben.

Across the table, she smiled at Robert. "You don't want to leave right away, do you?"

"Well . . . as soon as possible."

"But I wanted to see the studio. I can't come all the way across the Atlantic, and all the way down to Porthkerris and not see Ben's studio. Couldn't we drop in just for a moment, on the way back to London?"

This light-hearted suggestion was received in silence. Robert and Marcus both looked momentarily confused; Robert, because he did not want to put off any more time, and Marcus, because he knew that of all things, Ben hated to have his studio inspected. Emma also experienced a sinking of the heart. The studio was in chaos—not Ben's chaos which was of no account, but her own chaos. She thought of the step ladder, and the white-wash bucket, the wet towelling coat, and the bathing-suit which she had left abandoned on the floor, the brimming ashtrays, and the sagging sofa, and the sand everywhere. She looked at Ben, praying for him to refuse. They all looked at Ben, waiting like puppets, to see which way he would jerk the strings.

But for once he did not let them down.

"My dear Mrs. Ryan, despite the pleasure it would give me to show you my studio, I think I should point out that it is not on the way to London."

They all looked at her, to see how she would take this. But she merely pouted, and they laughed in relief, and Mrs. Ryan laughed too, with good grace.

"All right, I know when I'm beaten." She began to collect her bag and gloves. "But there is just one thing. You've all been so sweet to me, and I don't want to feel like a stranger any longer. My name's Melissa. Do you-all think you could manage to call me that?"

75

And later, when the men were loading the car, she got Emma to herself.

"You've been specially sweet," she said. "Marcus told me that you'd come back from Paris to be with your father, and here I am, taking him away from you again."

Emma, who knew that she had not been specially sweet, felt guilty. "The exhibition has to come first . . ."

"I'll take good care of him," Melissa Ryan promised.

Yes, thought Emma, *I'm sure you will*. And yet, despite herself, she liked the American woman. And there was something about the set of her chin and the clarity of her violet-blue eyes that made Emma wonder if perhaps, this time, Ben would not enjoy his usual walkover. And if things did not go his way from the very beginning he was apt to become discouraged. She smiled at Mrs. Ryan. She said, "I don't suppose it'll be long before he's home again." And she picked up the honey-coloured mink which lay across the back of a chair and helped Mrs. Ryan into it. They went out of the hotel together. It was colder now. The warmth of the sun had left the sky and a chill, like frost, swept up from the sea. Robert had put up the hood of the Alvis, and Melissa, wrapped in the mink, went to say goodbye to Ben.

"But it isn't goodbye," he told her, holding her hand, and gazing darkly down at her. "It's au revoir."

"Of course. And if you let me know when your flight arrives at Kennedy Airport, I'll arrange to have you met."

Marcus said, "I will do that. Ben has never in living memory let anybody know anything, least of all his time of arrival. Goodbye, Emma, my darling child, and don't forget that I have invited you to stay with us for as long as you like when Ben is in America."

"Bless you, Marcus. You never know. I might come."

They kissed. He got into the back of the car, and Melissa Ryan into the front, her elegant legs wrapped in Robert's car rug. Ben shut the door, then stooped to continue his conversation with her through the open window.

"Emma." It was Robert.

She turned. "Oh, goodbye, Robert."

To her surprise he took off his cap and bent to kiss her. "You'll be all right?"

She was touched. "Yes, of course."

"If you want anything, give me a ring, at Bernstein's."

"What could I want?"

"I don't know. Just a thought. Goodbye, Emma."

They stood, she and Ben, watching until the car had disappeared down the tunnel of trees. After it had gone, neither of them spoke, and then Ben cleared his throat, and said, portentously, as though he were giving a lecture, "What an interesting head that young man has. The narrow skull and the strong facial bones. I should like to see him with a beard. He would make a good saint—or perhaps, a sinner. Do you like him, Emma?"

She shrugged. "I suppose so. I scarcely know him."

He turned to move off, and caught sight of the small gathering of hotel guests, who, setting off for walks, or coming in from golf, or aimlessly snatching at the smallest straw of entertainment, had stayed to witness Melissa's departure. As Ben fixed them with his dark eyes, they became discomfited, turned away and moved on as though they had been caught doing something shameful.

He shook his head in amazement. "I think," he said, "I have had enough of being stared at as though I were a two-headed chimpanzee. Come along, we'll go home."

6

Ben Litton left for America at the end of March, travelling from Porthkerris to London via British Railways and from London to New York on a B.O.A.C. Boeing. At the last moment Marcus Bernstein decided to go with him, and the evening papers carried photographs of their departure, Ben with his white hair a coxcomb in the breeze, and Marcus almost obliterated by his black hat. Both looked faintly self-conscious.

It was from Marcus that Emma received the air mail bundle of American newspapers, carrying in their columns the comments of every worth-while art critic in the country. They were unanimous in their praise of the whole concept of the Queenstown Museum of Fine Arts, acclaiming it as a perfect example of architecture, lighting, and immaculate display. And the Ben Litton exhibition was on no account to be missed. Never again would the artist's work be available to the public in its entirety, and the two or three pre-war portraits, lent by private individuals, were alone worth a visit, if only to see how a single man could be painter, psychiatrist and absolving priest at one and the same time.

"Ben Litton uses his brush as a surgeon's scalpel, first laying bare the hidden sickness, then treating it with the utmost compassion."

The word compassion was used again for his war-time drawings, the shelter groups, the fire-fighters, and a handful of sketches salvaged from the time of the Allied advance in Italy. And of his post-war work they said, "Other painters abstract from nature. Litton abstracts from imagination, and an imagination so lively that it is difficult to believe that these vital paintings were not turned out by a man of half his age."

Emma read these and allowed herself to feel proud. The private view took place on the 3rd of April, and by the tenth there was still no word of Ben's return, but she filled in the days with time-consuming household chores, and eventually moved back to the studio to finish the white-washing. This took little mental concentration, and her mind wandered aimlessly into the future, indulging in the sort of day dreams that, a month ago, she would never have allowed herself. But now, she truly felt that things had changed. When she had gone to the station to put Ben on to the London train, he had kissed her goodbye—absentmindedly to be sure, as though he had forgotten for the moment who she was, but still, he had kissed her and that surely marked a milestone. And when he did eventually tear himself away from the adulation of the American public and returned to Porthkerris, she saw herself meeting the train, cool and composed, the perfect social secretary. And, maybe the next time he took off for some far-flung, but obviously colourful, corner of the globe, he would take Emma with him, and she would book flights, and see that he caught connections, and keep Marcus informed as to his movements.

And then, a day or two later, there was a letter from Marcus, postmarked London. She opened it hopefully, thinking that it would tell her that Ben was coming back, but, in fact, it was simply to say that Marcus had returned to London alone, and Ben had stayed in Queenstown.

The Ryan Memorial Museum is fascinating, and if I had been able, I should have stayed as well. It embraces all forms of art, has a small theatre and concert hall and a collection of Russian jewellery which has to be seen to be believed. Queenstown itself is charming, full of red brick Georgian houses, set in green lawns and veiled in flowering dogwood . . . they all look as though they have been there since the days of William and Mary, but in fact, I saw one in the process of being built, the mature lawn being laid in turves, and the dogwoods planted, fully grown. What it is to have a warm and temperate climate, to be sure.

Redlands (the Ryan homestead) is a great white house with a pillared "porch" where Ben sits in a long chair and gets brought mint juleps by a coloured butler called Henry. Henry comes to work each day in a lilac Chevrolet, and hopes, in the not-too-distant future, to become a lawyer. He is a bright young man and should achieve his ambition. There are also a couple of tennis courts—a paddock (corral) full of spirited horses, and the inevitable swimming-pool. Ben, as you can imagine, neither rides nor plays tennis, but spends long hours, when he isn't adding a little local colour to the retrospective exhibition, floating around the pool on a rubber mattress.

I am sorry that he has stayed away from you for so long, but honestly believe that he needs this rest. He has been working hard for the last few years, and a little harmless relaxation will do him no harm. If you are lonely, our invitation still stands. Come and stay with us. We should so love to have you.

Always your loving Marcus.

The white-washing was finished, the studio floor scrubbed. Ben's drawings had been stacked and stowed in numbered folios. His pens and brushes graded and various tubes of solidified oil paint, used once, and then abandoned, had been discreetly shovelled into the dustbin.

There was nothing left to do.

He had been gone two weeks when the postcard came from Christopher. Emma was in the kitchen of the cottage, making coffee and squeezing orange juice, still wrapped in her dressing-gown and with her hair tied back in a pony tail, when the postman, who was a cheeky young man in an open-necked shirt, put his head round the door and said, "Well, and how are you this morning, my handsome?"

"Splendid, thank you," said Emma, who had been putting up with this camaraderie ever since she returned from Paris.

He flapped a bundle of letters at her. "All for your old man. But . . . here . . . is a postcard for you." He inspected the picture before Emma snatched it from him. "So vulgar those things are; I don't know how decent folks can buy them."

"No, you wouldn't," said Emma rudely, scarcely glancing at the bulging lady in the bikini before turning the card over to see who it was from. The postmark was Brookford.

Emma darling, when are you coming to see me? I
can't come and see you, because we're up to the ears in
rehearsals for *Dead on Time*. Phone number Brookford
678, best about ten in the morning before we start work.
Producer nice chap, stage manager bloody, all girls have
spots, and not as pretty as you. Love Love Love Christo.

The nearest phone box was a mile away, so Emma went
down the street to the ramshackle grocer's where she bought
cigarettes and tins of food and soap flakes, and used the
telephone there.

It was an old-fashioned one, in two separate bits, and
with a hook that you jiggled to get the operator. She sat on a
beer crate and waited while the call was put through and a
grey and white cat, fat as a cushion, came and lay exhaust-
edly across her knee.

The phone was answered at last by a cross-sounding
female.

"Brookfield Theatre."

"Can I speak to Christopher Ferris?"

"I don't know if he's in yet."

"Could you go and look?"

"Oh, I suppose so. Who shall I say it is?"

"Say Emma."

The cross female departed. Various voices could be
heard, chattering. A man in the distance shouted, *"Here I
said, you clot, not there."* And then there were footsteps and
a voice, and it was Christo.

"Emma."

"You are there. They didn't know if you were in."

"Yes, of course I'm in . . . we're rehearsing in five
minutes . . . Did you get my postcard?"

"This morning."

"Did Ben read it?" (He obviously hoped that he had.)

"Ben isn't here. He's in America. I thought you'd know."

"How should I know?"

"It's been in all the papers."

"Actors don't read papers and if they do it's always the *Stage*. But if the old boy's in America, why didn't you let me know and come and stay with me?"

"For a hundred reasons."

"Name two."

"Well, he only meant to go for a week at the most; and I didn't know where you were."

"I told you. Brookford."

"I don't even know where Brookford is."

"Thirty-five minutes from London, trains run every half hour. Look, do come. Come and stay. I've been moved into a sinister basement flat. It smells of dry rot and old cats, but it's ever so cosy."

"Christo, I can't. I must be here. Ben'll be home any day now, and . . ."

"Did you tell him about meeting me again?"

"No, I didn't."

"Why not?"

"The subject never came up."

"You mean you were scared?"

"I was nothing of the sort. It was simply—irrelevant . . ."

"Nobody's ever called me irrelevant and got away with it. Oh, do come, ducky. My little basement nest needs the touch of a woman's hand. You know, scrubbing and all that jazz."

"I can't come till Ben's home. Then I'll try."

"It'll be too late by then. I'll have got it clean. Please. I'll get you a free ticket for the show. Or two tickets and you can bring a friend. Or three tickets and you can bring them all."

His voice dissolved into amusement. He had always laughed at his own jokes.

"Oh, very funny," said Emma, but she was laughing too.

"You're just playing hard to get. You wouldn't stay with me in Paris, and you won't come and keep house in the wilds of Surrey. What have I got to do to win your heart?"

"You won it years ago and you've had it ever since. Truthfully, I'm longing to see you. But I can't come. I simply can't come till Ben gets back."

Christo said a rude word.

The telephone went pip-pip-pip.

"That's it, then," Christo. "Let me know when you make up your mind. Goodbye."

"Goodbye, Christo." But he had already hung up. Smiling foolishly, going back over every word he had said, she put the receiver back on to the hook. The cat on her knee purred momentously, and Emma realised it was about to produce a family at any moment. An old man came into the shop to buy two ounces of plug, and when he had gone Emma picked up the cat and placed her gently on the floor, and felt in her pocket for loose change to pay for the call.

"When are the kittens due?" she asked.

The old woman behind the counter was called Gertie, and wore, indoors and out, an enormous brown beret pulled down over her eyebrows.

"Only time can tell, my dear." She put Emma's money into her till, which was an old tin box, and gave her her change. "Only time can tell."

"Thank you for letting me use your phone."

"It's a pleasure," said Gertie, who always listened, shamelessly, and relayed every word she heard.

* * *

In March it had been like midsummer. Now, in May, it was cold as November, and pouring with rain. He had never imagined Porthkerris in the rain; had always pictured it painted in the bright blues of summer, gay with the white wings of gulls and yachts, everything dazzling in a glaring sunlight. But now squalls, borne in on a cutting east wind, were flung against the windows of the hotel, sounding like fistfuls of pebbles. The gusts rattled the casements and then whined away beneath doors, down chimneys, blowing curtains, chilly and inescapable.

It was a Saturday, and Robert, flat on his bed, had been asleep. He looked at his watch and saw that it was five to three, so he reached for a cigarette, and lit it, and lay, watching the leaden sky race across the window, and waiting for the telephone to ring.

It did, at precisely three o'clock. He lifted the receiver.

"Three o'clock, sir," said the hall porter.

"Thank you very much."

"Sure you're awake, sir?"

"Yes. I'm awake."

He finished the cigarette, and stubbed it out, and got up, pulling on his white towel robe and heading for the bathroom for a hot shower. He hated sleeping in the afternoon, hated waking with the feeling that his teeth were itching, and that he was on the verge of a splitting headache, but after driving all through the night from London it had been impossible to stay awake. He had had an early lunch, and left word with the porter to call him. But the wind, blown up while he slept, had wakened him first.

He dressed, put on a clean shirt, tied his tie, picked up the jacket of his suit, and then changed his mind, and pulled on a polo-necked sweater instead. He combed his hair, slid his belongings from the top of the dressing table into his trouser pockets, took a raincoat from the back of the door and went downstairs.

The lounge was thick with the silence of mid-afternoon. Elderly residents snoozed, snoring lightly in dry heated air. Frustrated golfers watched the rain, rattling loose change in the pockets of their tweed knickerbockers, wondering if the weather was going to let up, if there would be time for nine holes before it got dark.

The hall porter took Robert's key and hung it up.

"Going out now, sir?"

"Yes, and perhaps you can help me. I want to get to the Society of Artists Gallery. I believe it's an old chapel, converted. Have you any idea where it is."

"That's down the old part of the town. Know your way round, do you?"

"I know the Sliding Tackle," said Robert, and the hall porter grinned. He liked a man who used pubs as landmarks.

"Well . . . say you're going to the Sliding Tackle, but turn up the street before you get there. Up, away from the harbour. Narrow little road, very steep, and there's a square at the head of it. Gallery's on the other side of the square. You can't miss it. Got great posters up outside . . . not that any living soul can make head nor tail of them . . ."

"Well, we'll have to see. Thank you very much."

"You're welcome." The porter swung the revolving door, and Robert was ejected into the bitter cold. Rain hammered at his unprotected head, he hunched himself into his raincoat, and picked his way across the gravel, trying to avoid the worst of the puddles. Inside, his car smelt damp and musty, an alien smell over the usual one of leather and cigarettes. He switched on the engine and the heater began to hum. A leaf was stuck in the blade of the windscreen wiper, but when he turned it on, the leaf was dislodged and torn from the wet glass by the wind.

He drove down to the town, and it was all deserted, abandoned, the inhabitants in a state of siege from the weather. Only a drenched policeman stood at point duty at the foot of the hill, and an old lady fought with an umbrella. The narrow streets acted as chimneys for the wind, which funnelled up them, cold and ferocious as a torrent of water, and when he came out on to the harbour road, he saw that the tide was full, and the harbour itself grey and choppy, fleeced with white-capped waves.

He found the street the porter had described. It climbed away from the harbour between crowded cottages, the cobbles wet and shining like the scales of a newly-caught fish. It crested the hill, and opened out into a picturesque square, and he saw the old chapel, a solid, gloomy building, quite at odds with the poster at its door.

PORTHKERRIS SOCIETY OF ARTISTS
SPRING EXHIBITION
Admission 5/-

Beneath this was a strange motif in purple—the suggestion of a staring eye, a six-fingered hand. Robert decided that he could see the hall porter's point of view.

He parked the car, and went up the streaming steps, and through the door, and was immediately assailed by the smell of a paraffin stove. He saw that the old chapel had been white-washed, the walls soared to high private windows, and liberally hung with every sort and size of painting.

Just inside the door, her knees covered with a rug, sat a lady in a felt hat. On one side of her was a wooden table, with catalogues and a bowl for money, on the other was the paraffin heater, at which she was trying to warm a pair of purple-knuckled hands.

"Oh, close the door, close the door," she implored as

87

Robert blew in on a gust of wind. He leaned against the door, shutting it, and feeling in his trouser pocket for two half-crowns. "What a freezing day," she went on, "and this is meant to be summer. You're my first visitor this afternoon. You are a visitor, aren't you? I haven't seen your face around the place."

"No, I haven't been here before."

"We've got a most interesting collection—you'll have a catalogue, of course. Another half-crown, please. But I think you'll agree, well worth it."

"Thank you," said Robert, feebly.

He took the catalogue, decorated with the same purple hand-and-eye motif as the poster outside, and opened it casually, running his eye down the list of artists for the name he wanted.

". . . er . . . any particular artist?" The woman at the desk managed to sound diffident, but she had an inquisitive gleam in her eye.

"No . . . not really."

"Just generally interested, I expect. Are you staying in Porthkerris?"

"Yes . . ." he began to move away from her. "For the moment I am."

He took it slowly, pacing down the long room, feigning interest in every picture. He had found the name, Pat Farnaby. Number 24. The Journey, by Pat Farnaby. He stayed a long time at number 23, then moved on again.

The colour pounced at him. There was a sensation of great height, a dizzying sensation, like vertigo. And yet with it, a sense of elation, as though he were above the clouds, caught, suspended, between the blue and the white.

You must go, Marcus had said. *I want you to form an opinion of your own. You can't remain the man who keeps the*

books for the rest of your life. Besides, I'd like to see your
reaction.

And this was it. This pure, high note of simple colour.

After a little, he went back to the persistent lady. He
was aware that all the time she had been watching him.
Now, he thought, she was bright-eyed as a greedy robin,
waiting for a bread crumb.

"Is that Pat Farnaby's only exhibit?"

"I'm afraid so. It was all we could persuade him to let
us have."

"He lives around here, doesn't he?"

"Oh, yes. Out at Gollan."

"Gollan?"

"That's about six miles away, out on the moor road. It's
a farm."

"You mean he's a farmer?"

"Oh, no." She laughed. *Merrily*, thought Robert, as
though she were following the directions in an old-fashioned
play. "He lives in the loft over the barn. Here," she drew a
scrap of paper towards her, wrote an address. "If you want to
see him, I'm sure you'll find him here."

He took the paper. "Thank you very much." He started
for the door.

"But don't you want to look at the rest of our exhibition?"

"Another time, perhaps."

"It's so *interesting*." She sounded as though her heart
would break if he did not look at some more pictures.

"Yes, I'm sure. But another time." It was at this moment
that he thought of Emma Litton. His hand on the doorknob,
he turned back. "By the way, if I wanted to find Ben Litton's
house . . . is it near here? The house, I mean, not the studio?"

"Well, of course, it's just round the corner. About a

hundred yards down the road. It's got a blue gate. You can't miss it. But you do know that Mr. Litton's not at home?"

"Yes, I know."

"He's in America."

"Yes, I know that, too."

It was still streaming with rain. He got back into the car, and started the engine, and nosed it forward down a street as narrow as a burrow. At the blue gate he left it, parked, completely filling the road, and went through the gate, and down a flight of steps which led to a flagged court-yard where tubs stood, filled with drowned-looking plants, and a painted wooden seat disintegrated slowly in the damp. The house itself was long and low, single-storied, but the uneven roofs and ill-matched chimney pots indicated that it had once been two small cottages, or even three. The front door was painted blue to match the gate, and had a copper dolphin as a knocker.

Robert knocked. From above a stream of water poured down upon him from a faulty gutter. He stepped back and looked up to see where it came from, and as he did so, the door was opened.

He said, "Good afternoon. Your gutter's leaking."

"Where on *earth* have you sprung from?"

"London. You should get it mended or it'll rust away."

"Have you come all the way from London to tell me that?"

"No, of course I haven't. Can I come in?"

"Of course . . ." She stood back, holding the door open for him. "But you are the most disconcerting man. You keep just turning up, with no notice at all."

"How can we give you notice if you aren't on the telephone? And there wasn't time to write a letter."

"Is it about Ben?"

Robert went into the house, ducking his head beneath the lintel of the door, unbuttoning his wet raincoat.

"No. Should it be?"

"I thought he might be home."

"As far as I know he's still basking in that balmy Virginia sunshine."

"Well, then?"

He turned to face her. It occurred to him then that in an odd way she was unpredictable as the weather itself. Each time he met up with her, she seemed a different person. To-day she wore a dress in red and orange stripes, and long black stockings. Her hair had been caught back on the nape of her neck with a tortoiseshell slide, and her fringe had grown. It was too long, it would get into her eyes, give her a squint. As he watched her, she pushed it back, off her face, with the heel of her hand. It was a gesture both defensive and disarming and it made her seem very young.

He took the scrap of paper out of his pocket and handed it across to her. Emma read it aloud.

"Pat Farnaby, Gollan Home Farm." She looked up at him. "But where did you get this?"

"From the female at the Art Gallery."

"Pat Farnaby?"

"Marcus is interested."

"Why didn't he come himself?"

"He wanted a second opinion. Mine."

"Have you formed one?"

"It's difficult to say after seeing only a single painting. I thought I might be able to see some more."

Emma said warningly, "He's a very odd young man."

"I should expect him to be. Do you know where Gollan is?"

"Of course. It belongs to Mr. and Mrs. Stevens. We

used to go out in summer for picnics on the cliffs. But I haven't been since I got back this time."

"Will you come with me now? Show me the way?"

"How do we get there?"

"The car's outside. I drove down from London last night."

"You must be exhausted."

"No, I've had a sleep."

"Where are you staying?"

"At the hotel. Can you come? Now?"

"Of course."

"You'll need a coat."

Emma smiled at him. "If you can spare thirty seconds, I'll get one."

When she had gone, her footsteps clattering away down an uncarpeted passage, Robert lit a cigarette and stood, looking about him, intrigued not only by the oddly-shaped little house, but also because it represented the unfamiliar, domestic side of Ben Litton's stormy personality.

The blue front door had led them straight into the living-room, low ceilinged and darkly beamed. There was a huge window with a view of the sea, its deep sill crowded with indoor plants—geraniums and ivy and a Victorian jug full of pink roses. The floor was flagged with slate and scattered with bright rugs, and there were books and magazines everywhere, and a great deal of blue and white Spanish pottery. In a granite hearth, flush with the floor, a log fire smouldered, flanked by baskets of weathered driftwood, and over this hung the only picture in the room.

His professional eye had noticed this as soon as he came into the house, but now Robert went over to inspect it more closely. It was a large oil of a child on a donkey. She wore a red dress, carried a bunch of white daisies, wore a garland of them on her dark head. The donkey stood knee-deep in the lush grass of summer, and, far beyond, the sea and the sky were suffused by a haze of fine weather. The child's dangling feet were bare, her eyes pale in the brown bloom of her face.

Emma Litton, by her father. Robert wondered when it had been painted.

The wind rose, with a sudden witch's shriek, and flung a torrent of rain at the window. It was an eerie sound and he realised that this could be a lonely place to live, and wondered what Emma found to do on such a day. When she came back, carrying her coat and a pair of gum boots, which she proceeded to pull on, he asked her about this.

"Oh, I clean the house, and I cook things and I go and shop. It all takes quite a long time."

"And this afternoon? What were you doing this afternoon when I knocked on the door?"

Emma tugged at the gumboot. "I was ironing."

"And what about evenings? What do you do in the evenings?"

"I usually go out. I go for walks and things. I watch the gulls and the cormorants. I look at the sunset, pick up driftwood for the fire."

"Alone? Haven't you got any friends?"

"Oh, yes, but the children who lived here when I was little have all grown up and gone away."

It sounded bleak. On an impulse, Robert said, "You could come back to London with me. Helen would love to have you."

"Yes, I know she would, but it's hardly worth it, is it? After all, Ben'll be back any day now. It's only a matter of days."

She began to pull on her coat. It was navy blue and, with her black stockings and gum boots, made her look like a schoolgirl.

"Have you had any word from Ben?" Robert asked.

"From Ben? You must be joking."

"I'm beginning to wish we'd never suggested he went back to America."

"Why?"

"Because it doesn't seem fair on you."

"Oh, heavens, I'm all right." She smiled. "Shall we go?"

The Stevens' farm lay in a grey stretch of moor that swept down to the cliffs. Grey, lichened, sunk like a boulder into the land, it might have been simply another larger outcrop of granite. The lane which led down from the road wound deep between tall stone hedges, crowned with hawthorn and brambles. The car bumped and jolted down the track, crossed a small bridge, came to the first cottages, a flock of white geese, and finally the farmyard, shrill with the voice of a screaming cockerel.

Robert stopped the car and switched off the engine. The wind was dying, the rain seemed to have congealed into a sea-mist, thick as smoke. There were various farm sounds; cows lowing, hens clucking, the distant churning of a tractor.

"Now," said Robert, "how do I find this man?"

"He lives in the loft of that barn . . . you go up the stone steps to his door."

The stone steps were already occupied by a number of wet hens, pecking for scraps of grain, and a bored-looking tabby cat. Below them, in the mud of the yard, a huge sow was rootling about. There was a strong smell of manure. Robert sighed. "The things I am expected to do, and all in the name of Art." He opened the door of the car and began to get out. "Do you want to come?"

"I think I'd be more use out of the way."

"I'll try not to be too long."

She watched him pick his way across the sodden farm yard, toe the pig aside, cautiously climb the steps. He knocked on the door, and then, when there was no reply, opened it and stepped inside. The door shut behind him. Almost at once another door opened, in the farmhouse this time, and the farmer's wife emerged, in boots and a raincoat to her ankles, and a black sou'wester. She carried a stout stick and came down the garden path, peering through the rain to see who was in the big green car.

Emma rolled down the window. "Hello, Mrs. Stevens. It's me."

"Who?"

"Emma Litton."

Mrs. Stevens broke into a cackle of delighted astonishment, slapped her side, put her hand over her heart. "Emma! Well, what a surprise you gave me. I haven't seen you since goodness knows how long. What are you doing here?"

"I came out with a man who wants to see Pat Farnaby. He's up there now."

"Is your father home yet?"

"No, he's still in America."

"On your own, are you?"

"That's right. How's Ernie?" Ernie was Mr. Stevens.

"He's lovely, but had to go into town to-day to see the dentist about his plate. Agony, it gives him, he can scarcely bear to keep it in his mouth. That's why I'm getting the cows in for him . . ."

On an impulse Emma said, "I'll come with you . . ."

"Too wet for you."

"I've got boots . . . besides, I'd like the walk." She liked Mrs. Stevens, too, a woman who remained unquenchably cheerful under all circumstances. They climbed a stile and started out over the sodden fields. "You've been abroad, haven't you?" said Mrs. Stevens. "Yes, I thought you had. I never knew you were home. Pity your Daddy had to go off like this. Still, can't be helped, I suppose, him being the sort of man he is . . ."

The interview with Pat Farnaby was a difficult one, to say the least of it. He was an intense young man, very pale and undernourished, with a shock of carrotty hair and a beard to match. His eyes were green and suspicious as a hungry cat's, and he appeared to be very dirty. His abode was also dirty, but this Robert had expected and, accordingly, ignored.

What he had not expected, though, was such antagonism. Pat Farnaby did not like strangers walking in, uninvited and unannounced, when he was working. Robert apologised and explained that he had come on business, whereupon the young man simply asked Robert what he was trying to sell.

Beating down his irritation, Robert tried another tack. With some ceremony, he produced Marcus Bernstein's card. "Mr. Bernstein asked me to come and see you, perhaps to look at your work, find out what your plans are . . ."

"I haven't any plans," said the artist. "I never make plans." He treated the card as though it were contaminated and must not be touched, so that Robert was forced to put it down on the corner of a littered table.

"I saw your picture at the gallery in Porthkerris, but it is only one picture."

"So what?"

Robert cleared his throat. Marcus was infinitely better at dealing with this sort of thing, and Marcus never lost his temper. It took time to cultivate such patience, Robert knew. His own was slipping away, like greasy rope between his fingers. He took a firm grip of it.

"I'd like to see some more of your work."

Pat Farnaby's pale eyes narrowed. "How did you find me?" he asked, sounding like a cornered criminal.

"They gave me your address at the gallery. Emma Litton came with me to show me the way. Perhaps you know Emma."

"I've seen her around."

They seemed to be getting nowhere. In the silence that followed Robert let his his eyes travel over the unsavoury studio. There were only the most sordid signs of human habitation; a bed like a disintegrating nest, a dirty frying pan, some nasty socks soaking in a bucket, an opened tin of beans, the jagged edge of the lid sticking up. But there were also many canvasses, stacked, scattered, propped on chairs, against walls. A potential treasure trove. Anxious beyond belief to inspect them, he dragged his eyes back to meet the cold unwinking stare of the artist.

He said at last, gently, "Mr. Farnaby, I haven't all the time in the world."

Put to the test, Pat Farnaby's resistance cracked. He seemed, all at once, unsure of himself. Arrogance and rudeness were his only defences against the whims of a more sophisticated world. He scratched his head, frowned, made a face of resignation, and at last went to lift a random canvas and turn it to face the light.

"There's this," he said uncertainly, and backed away from it to stand by Robert. As he did so, Robert took a new packet of cigarettes from his pocket and handed them across to the young man. In the silence that followed, Pat Farnaby cautiously slit the cellophane wrapper, took out a cigarette and lit it, and then, with the stealthy movements of a man who does not wish to be observed, slid the packet into his own trouser pocket.

* * *

An hour later Robert returned to the car. Emma, waiting for him, saw him come down the steps of the barn, pick his way across the farmyard. She leaned across to open the door for him, and as he got in beside her, asked, "How did you get on?"

"I think all right." He sounded cautious, but excited.

"Did he show you his work?"

"Most of it."

"And it's good?"

"I think so. We may be on the verge of something enormously important, but it's all in such an appalling mess that it's hard to be sure. Nothing's framed, there's no sequence or order . . ."

"I was right, wasn't I? He's a real odd-ball?"

"Crazy," said Robert. He grinned at her. "But a genius."

He turned the car in the yard and headed back up the lane towards the road. He was whistling tunelessly through his teeth and Emma sensed, beneath his excitement, the satisfaction of a job well done.

She said, "You'll want to speak to Marcus now."

"I said I'd telephone right away." He eased his cuff from the face of his watch, checked on the time. "A quarter past six. He said he'd wait in the Gallery till seven and then go home."

"If you like, you can drop me at the crossroads and I'll walk home."

"Now, why should I do that?"

"I haven't got a telephone, and you'll want to hurry back to the hotel."

He smiled. "It's not as urgent as all that. And if it hadn't been for you, I'd probably still be looking for Pat Farnaby. The least I can do is to take you home."

They were on the moor now, high above the sea. The wind had eased off considerably, veering round to the west, and ahead the sky seemed to be opening and breaking up, and there were unexpected scraps of blue, growing larger every moment, and watery fingers of sunlight. Emma said, "It's going to be a lovely evening," and as she spoke was conscious that she did not want Robert to go back to the hotel and leave her to spend it on her own. He had blown, unexpectedly, into the gloomy day, given it shape and purpose, filled with companionship of a shared venture, and now she did not want it to end.

She said, "When are you going back to London?"

"To-morrow morning. Sunday. Back in the Gallery Monday morning. It's been a full week-end."

So there was only this evening. She imagined him telephoning Marcus from the phone by his bed. Then he would have a bath, perhaps a drink, go down for dinner. On Saturday evenings the Castle Hotel held little dinner dances; there was a band in white mess jackets and a patch of floor cleared for dancing. Deeply influenced by Ben, Emma had been brought up to regard such functions as unbearably genteel and boring, but to-night she felt that it would be fun to let Ben's rigid opinions go to the devil. She yearned for the starched white table cloths, the last year's hit tunes, the ritual of the wine list, the souped-up glamour of pink-shaded lights.

Beside her Robert spoke unexpectedly, interrupting her train of thought.

"When did your father paint the picture of you on the donkey?"

"Why did you suddenly ask that?"

"I was thinking about it. It's enchanting. You look so solemn and important."

"That's the way I felt, solemn and important. I was six,

99

and it was the only painting he ever did of me. The donkey was called Mokey. He used to carry us up and down to the beach along with all the picnic baskets and things."

"Have you always lived in the cottage?"

"Not always. Just since Ben married Hester. Before that we used to stay anywhere—in boarding-houses, or with friends. Sometimes we just camped in the Studio. It was rather fun. But Hester said she had no intention of living like a gipsy, so she bought the cottages and converted them."

"She did a good job."

"Yes, she was clever. But Ben has never thought of that house as home. His home is his Studio and when he's in Porthkerris, he spends as little time as possible in the cottage. I think its associations with Harriet slightly get him down. He's always expecting her to walk in and tell him that he's late for something, or that he's tracking mud on to the floor, or he's putting paint on the sofa cushions . . ."

"The creative instinct seems to thrive in disorder."

Emma laughed. "Do you suppose, that when you and Marcus have made Pat Farnaby rich and famous, he will still want to roost with Mrs. Stevens' chickens?"

"That remains to be seen. But if he does come to London, there's no doubt that somebody will have to scrub him down and comb the dust of ages out of that scrofulous beard. Still . . ." He stretched luxuriously, arching his back against the leather seat. "It'll be worth it."

They had crested the hill and were now running down the long road that led to Porthkerris. The sea, in the calm evening light, had turned the translucent blue of butterfly wings; the tide was out, and the great bay an arc of newly-washed sand. The rain had left everything sparkling and fresh, and as the moors and the fields fell behind them, and they drove down through the narrow streets, Emma saw windows flung open to the fresh evening air, and caught, from tiny stamp-sized gardens, the heady smells of roses and lilac.

And there were other smells, too. Saturday evening smells, of fish frying and cheap scent. And there were people strolling the pavements in their best clothes, a smattering of early summer visitors, and boys and girls, hand in hand, headed for the cinema and the little cafés that lined the harbour road.

Stopped at the cross roads by the point-duty policeman, Robert observed them.

"What does young love do in Porthkerris on Saturday night, Emma?"

"It depends on the weather."

The policeman waved them on.

"What are we going to do?" asked Robert.

"We?"

"Yes. You and I. Do you want to be taken out for dinner?"

For a mad moment Emma wondered if she had been yearning aloud. "Well . . . I . . . you don't have to feel you have to . . ."

"I don't feel I have to. I want to. I'd like to. Where shall we go? My hotel? Or would you hate that?"

"No . . . of course . . . I wouldn't hate it . . ."

"Perhaps you've got some amusing little Italian place you like better."

"There aren't any amusing little Italian places in Porthkerris."

"No, I was afraid there wouldn't be. So it'll have to be the palm court and the central heating."

"There's a band too," said Emma, feeling she should warn him. "On Saturday nights. And people dance."

"You make it sound indecent."

"I thought perhaps you disliked that sort of thing. Ben does."

"I don't dislike it at all. Like most things, it can be quite fun if you do it with the right person."

"I never thought of it that way."

Robert laughed and looked again at his watch. "Half past six. I'll take you home, then go back to the hotel and change, and speak to Marcus, and then come back for you. Would half past seven be time enough?"

"I'll give you a drink," said Emma. "There's a bottle of Uncle Remus' Genuine Ole Rye Whisky that Ben was given ten years ago, and it's still not been opened. I've always longed to see what was inside."

But Robert was unenthusiastic. "Perhaps I'd better just make a Martini."

At the hotel he collected his key, and three messages with it.

"When did these come?"

"The times are noted, sir. Three forty-five, five o'clock, half-past-five. A Mr. Bernstein, telephoning from London. He says to call him the moment you come in."

"I was going to do that anyway; but thanks."

Frowning a little, for such impatience was foreign to Marcus, Robert went upstairs to his room. The copious telephone calls were disturbing. He wondered if Marcus had heard rumors that some other Gallery was after the young artist. Or perhaps he had had second thoughts about Farnaby's work, and wanted to cancel the whole thing.

In his room, the curtains had been drawn, the bed turned down, the fire turned on. He sat on the bed, and picked up the receiver and gave the number of the Gallery. He took the three telephone messages out of his pocket and put them in a neat row on top of the beside table. *Mr. Bern-*

*stein would like you to call him. Mr. Bernstein called, will
ring later. Mr. Bernstein . . .*

"Kent 3778. Bernstein Galleries."

"Marcus . . ."

"Robert, thank God I've got you at last. Did you get my
message?"

"Three of them. But I said I would call you about
Farnaby."

"This isn't about Farnaby. This is much more important.
This is about Ben Litton."

There was a dress, seen in Paris, wildly expensive, cov-
eted, and finally bought. It was black, sleeveless, very plain.
"But when will you wear such a dress?" Madame Duprés
had asked, and Emma, basking in the luxury of possession,
had replied, "Oh, some time. Some special time."

There had never been such an occasion until tonight.
Now, with her hair coiled high and pearl earstuds set in her
ears, Emma drew the black dress carefully over her head,
zipped it up and fastened the tiny belt, and her reflection in
the mirror reassured her that all those thousands of francs
had been well-spent.

When Robert came, she was in the kitchen, struggling
with a trayful of ice-cubes for the Martinis that he had promised to make. She heard his car, the slam of the door, the
gate open and shut and his footsteps as he ran down the
steps, and in a panic, she tumbled the ice into a glass dish
and went to let him in, and found that the sullen day had
turned into a clear and perfect night, jewel-blue and scattered with stars.

In surprise, she said, "What a beautiful night."

"Amazing, isn't it? After all that wind and rain Porthkerris is looking like Positano." He came into the house and
Emma closed the door behind him. "There's even a moon

rising over the sea to complete the illusion. All we need now is a guitar and a tenor singing Santa Lucia."

"Perhaps we'll find one."

He had changed into a dark grey suit, a starched shirt with an impeccable collar and a gleam of white cuff, linked with gold, showing at his wrist. His tawny hair was once more tamed and smoothly brushed, and he brought with him the crisp, lemony smell of after-shave.

"Do you still want to make a Martini? I've got everything ready, I was just trying to get the ice . . ." She went back to the kitchen, raising her voice to talk through the open door. "The gin and the Martini are on the table and a lemon. Oh, and you'll need a knife to cut the lemon with."

She opened a drawer and found one, pointed and very sharp, and she carried the knife and the bowl of ice back into the living-room. "What a pity Ben isn't here. He adores Martinis, only he can never remember the right proportions and he always drowns them with lemon . . ."

Robert made no reply to this. It occurred then to Emma that he had made no effort to make himself at home. He had done nothing about their drinks, he had not even lit himself a cigarette, and this in itself was unusual, for he was normally the most relaxed and composed of men. But now there was a definite constraint about him, and with a sinking heart, Emma wondered if he was already regretting the evening they were to spend together.

She went to put the lemon down beside the empty glasses, told herself she was imagining things, turned to swiftly smile at him. "Now, what else do you need?"

"Not another thing," said Robert, and put his hands into his trouser pockets. *Not the gesture of a man who is about to make a Martini.* In the fire a burning log settled and broke, sending up a shower of sparks.

Perhaps it was the telephone call that had upset him. "Did you speak to Marcus?"

"Yes, I did. As a matter of fact, he'd been trying to get me on the telephone most of the afternoon."

"And of course you were out. Was he pleased when you told him about Pat Farnaby?"

"He wasn't calling about Farnaby."

"He wasn't?" Suddenly she was afraid. "Is it bad news?"

"No, of course not, but you may not be very pleased. It's about your father. You see, he called Marcus this morning, from the States. He wanted Marcus to tell you that yesterday, in Queenstown, he and Melissa Ryan were married."

Emma realised that she was still holding the knife, that it was very sharp and that she might cut herself with it, so she set it down, very carefully, alongside the lemon . . .

Married. The word conjured up a hysterical image of a wedding; of Ben with a white flower in the button-hole of his sagging corduroy jacket; of Melissa Ryan in her pink wool suit, misted in white veiling and paper confetti; of demented Church bells jangling their message out across the verdant Virginia countryside that Emma had never seen. It was like a nightmare.

She realised that Robert Morrow was still talking, his voice even and calm.

". . . Marcus feels that in some obscure way, he is to blame. Because he thought the private view was a good idea, and because he was with them in Queenstown—he saw them together all the time, and he never had the faintest inkling that this was going to happen."

Emma remembered Marcus' description of the beautiful house, saw Ben caged by Melissa's money, a pacing tiger with all his creative impulses smothered by luxury; and she

105

realised that she had underestimated Melissa Ryan in imagining that Ben would be put off by having to fight for what he wanted. She had not appreciated how much he would want it.

Suddenly, she was angry. "He should never have gone back to America. There was no need. He simply wanted to be left alone and to get on with his painting."

"Emma, nobody made him go."

"It isn't as though the marriage will last. Ben's never stayed faithful to a woman longer than six months, and I can't see Melissa Ryan standing for that."

Robert said mildly, "Perhaps this time it will work, and it will last."

"But you saw them together that day they met. They couldn't keep their eyes off each other. If she had been old and ugly, nothing would have dragged him away from Porthkerris."

"But she wasn't old and ugly. She's very beautiful, and highly intelligent and very rich. And if it hadn't been Melissa Ryan, very soon it would have been somebody else, and what is more . . ." he went on, swiftly, before Emma could interrupt, ". . . you know as well as I do that that is true."

She said bitterly, "But at least we would have had more than a month together."

Hopelessly, Robert shook his head. "Oh, Emma, let him go."

His tone infuriated her. "He's my father. What's wrong in wanting to be with him?"

"He's not a father, any more than he's a husband or a lover or a friend. He's an artist. As that dedicated maniac we went to see this afternoon is an artist. They have no time for our values or standards. Everything, and everybody else, has to take second place."

"*Second* place? I wouldn't mind taking second place, or

third, or fourth. But I've always come at the bottom of a long list of priorities. His painting, his love affairs, his perpetual shunting about all over the world; even Marcus, and you. You're all more important to Ben than ever I was."

"Then leave him alone. Think about something else for a change. Chuck all this, leave it behind. Get yourself a job."

"I've done all those things. I've been doing them for the past two years."

"Then come back to London with me to-morrow and stay with Marcus and Helen. It'll get you away from Porthkerris, give you time to get used to the idea of Ben being married again, decide what you want to do next."

"Perhaps I've already decided."

It was there, in the back of her mind. Like watching the revolving stage from the darkened auditorium of a theatre. One set moves out of sight and as it does the new scenery comes slowly on to the stage. A different set. Another room, perhaps. Another view from another window. "But I don't want to come to London."

"And this evening?"

Emma frowned. She had forgotten. "This evening?"

"We're having dinner together."

She felt that she could not bear it. "I really would rather not . . ."

"It'll do you good . . ."

"No it won't. And I've got a headache . . ." It was an excuse, made-up, and it was with astonishment that she realised it was true. A pain that felt like the start of a migraine, with her eyeballs dragged by wires into the back of her head; the thought of food, chicken in gravy, ice-cream, was nauseous. "I couldn't come. I couldn't."

Robert said gently, "It isn't the end of the world," and the old, comforting cliché was somehow more than Emma could take. To her horror, she began to cry. She covered her face with her hands, pressing her finger tips into her thudding scalp, trying to stop, knowing that crying would make it worse, that she would be blinded with pain, that she would be sick . . .

She heard him say her name, and in two strides he had covered the space between them, and he put his arms around her, cradling her, letting her cry all over the immaculate grey lapels of his good suit. And Emma did not try to move away, but stayed still, tightly clenched against her own grief, rigid and unresponsive and hating him for what he had done to her.

7

Jane Marshall, her hand curved round a half full tumbler of Scotch-on-the-rocks, said, ". . . so what happened then?"

"Nothing happened. She didn't want to come out to dinner, and she looked as though she was going to have a bilious attack, so I put her to bed, and gave her a hot drink and an aspirin, and then I went back to the hotel and had dinner on my own. Then, the next morning, the Sunday, I went down to the cottage to say good-bye before I drove back to London. She was up and about, rather pale, but she seemed to be all right."

"Did you try again to make her come back with you?"

"Yes, I did, but she was adamant. So we said good-bye, and I left her. And since then there has been no word."

"But you can surely find out where she is?"

"There is no way of finding out. There's no telephone, never has been. Marcus wrote, of course, but Emma seems to have inherited Ben's built-in aversion to answering letters. There hasn't been another word."

"But this is crazy. In this day and age . . . there must be someone who can tell you . . ."

"There's no-one. No-one Emma ever talked to. There was no daily woman, coming in to clean, she did it all herself. That was the big reason for going back to Porthkerris in the first place, so that she could keep house for Ben. Of course, after two weeks of frigid silence, Marcus could stand it no longer, and put through a telephone call to the landlord of the Sliding Tackle, which was the pub Ben used to frequent, but Ben had been gone for six weeks, anyway, and Emma never went near the place."

"Then you'll have to go down to Porthkerris and ask around."

"Marcus isn't prepared to do that."

"Why not?"

"For reasons. Emma isn't a child. She's been hurt, and Marcus respects the fact that if she wants to be left alone, he has no right to interfere. He's asked her to come to London and live with Helen and himself . . . anyway until she's found her feet again. He can scarcely do more. And there's another reason, too."

"I know," said Jane. "It's Helen, isn't it?"

"Yes, it is," said Robert, hating to admit it. "Helen has always resented the hold Ben has over Marcus. There have been times when she would gladly have seen Ben at the bottom of the ocean. But she's accepted it because she had to, because wet-nursing Ben's career is part of Marcus's job, and without Marcus to keep him, more or less on the rails, God knows what would have happened to Ben Litton."

"And now she doesn't want him to start killing himself over Emma."

"Precisely."

Jane rocked her glass, letting the ice clink against its side. She said, "And you?"

He looked up. "What about me?"

"Do you feel involved?"

"Why do you ask that?"

"You sound involved."

"I scarcely know the girl."

"But you're worried about her."

He considered this. "Yes," he said at last. "Yes, I suppose I am. God knows why."

His glass was empty. Jane laid down her own drink, and got up to take his glass and pour him another whisky. From behind him, busy with ice, she said, "Why don't *you* go down to Porthkerris and find out?"

"Because she isn't there."

"She isn't . . . ? You know? But you never told me that."

"After the abortive telephone call to the Sliding Tackle, Marcus got the wind up. He rang the local police, and they found out a few facts and called us back. Cottage closed up, studio closed up, Post Office told to keep all mail until further notice." He reached up to take the fresh drink that Jane handed him over the back of the sofa. "Thanks."

"And her father . . . ? Does he know?"

"Yes, Marcus wrote and told him. But you can't expect Ben to get unduly excited. After all, he's still in the throes of what is virtually a honeymoon, and Emma's been sculling round Europe on her own since she was fourteen. Don't forget, that this is not a normal father-daughter relationship"

Jane sighed. "It most certainly isn't."

Robert grinned at her. She was a comfortingly down-to-earth person and it was for this reason that, on an impulse, he had dropped in this evening for a drink on his way home from work. Usually, the double life he led with Marcus Bernstein, working with him at the Gallery, as well as living in the same house, offered no strain at all. But just now, things were difficult. Robert had come back from a business trip to Paris, to find Marcus on edge, and unable to concentrate for very long on anything but the problem of Emma Litton. After discussing it with him, Robert realised that Marcus blamed himself for what had happened, and refused to be talked out of his guilt. Helen, on the other hand, was unsympathetic, and determined that he should not get himself more deeply involved in the whole sorry business, and for the moment the tensions had got on top of them, and split the menage at Milton Gardens from top to bottom.

The situation was not improved by the weather. After a cool spring, London had suddenly been caught up on the throes of a veritable heatwave. The early mornings broke in a pearl-like mist which gradually dissolved into day after day of baking sun. Girls went to work in sleeveless dresses, men shed their jackets and sat at their desks in shirt sleeves. The parks at lunchtime were filled with recumbent picnickers; shops and restaurants sprouted striped awnings, windows were flung open to the smallest breeze, and in the streets, parked cars frizzled and pavements glared, and melted tar stuck to the soles of shoes.

The heat, like some monstrous epidemic, had invaded even the quiet, pond-green recesses of the Bernstein Gallery. All day long there had been an endless stream of visitors and prospective clients, for the trans-Atlantic tourist season had started, and this was apt to be their busiest time. And at the end of it all, Robert, driving home, had found himself longing for a new face, a cool drink, and some conversation that had nothing to do with Artists, be they Renaissance, Impressionist or Pop.

Jane Marshall sprang immediately to mind.

Her little house was in a narrow mews between Sloane Square and the Pimlico Road. As he turned the car into the street, and eased down over the cobbles, he gave a double toot on the horn, and she appeared at the open upstairs window, her hands on the sill, her fair hair falling over her face as she leaned out to see who it was.

"Robert! I thought you were still in Paris."

"I was till two days ago. Have you got such a thing as a long, cool, alcoholic drink for an exhausted working man?"

"Of course I have. Hold on. I'll come down and let you in."

Her tiny house had always charmed him. Originally a coachman's cottage, it had a steep, narrow stair, which led straight up to the first floor. Here there was an open hallway, a sitting-room, and a kitchen, and upstairs again, in the slope-roofed loft, her bedroom and bathroom. As such it was inadequate enough, but since she had started her interior decorating business, it had become a joke. The sitting-room she had turned into a workroom, but still the bales of fabric, the fringing and the cushions, and the small bits of bric-àbrac she so cleverly picked up, overflowed into every available corner of space, rendering it all as gay and colourful as a patchwork quilt.

She was delighted to see him. She had spent the morning with a tiresome woman who wanted her entire house in St. John's Wood done up in cream, which she called "Redecorating in Magnolia." And then there had been a session with a young and rising actress who demanded something startling for her new flat.

113

"She sat here for hours, showing me pictures of the sort of thing she had in mind. I tried to tell her she should get a bulldozer in, not an interior decorator, but she wouldn't listen. These people never do. Whisky?"

"That," said Robert, collapsing on the sofa in front of the open window, "is the nicest thing anybody has said to me all day."

She poured two drinks, made sure he was supplied with cigarettes and an ashtray, and then settled herself composedly down to face him. She was a very pretty girl. Her blonde hair was straight and thick, cut in a curve to her chin. Her eyes were green, her nose tip-tilted, her mouth sweet, but implacable. Her broken marriage had left certain scars upon her character and she was not always the most tolerant of people, but there was a directness about her that he found as refreshing as a drink of cold water, and she always looked delicious.

Now he said, "I came here with the express purpose of not talking shop. How did we get on to the subject of Ben Litton anyway?"

"I brought it up. I was intrigued. Every time I saw Helen, she kept dropping maddening hints and then refusing to say more. She feels strongly about this, doesn't she?"

"Only because, in his day, Ben Litton has run poor Marcus ragged."

"Does she know Emma?"

"She hasn't seen her since she went to Switzerland six years ago."

"It's difficult," said Jane, "to be fair about people if you don't know them very well."

"It's sometimes difficult to be fair even if you do. And now . . ." He leaned forward to stub out his cigarette. "Let's drop the subject and make a tacit agreement not to mention it again. Are you doing anything this evening?"

"Not a thing."

"Then why don't we go and find somewhere with a roof garden or a terrace, and have a quiet dinner together?"

"I'd like that," said Jane.

"I'll call Helen and tell her I'm not coming back . . ."

"In that case . . ." She stood up. "I shall go and have a shower and change. I shan't be long."

"There isn't any hurry."

"Make yourself at home . . . get yourself another drink. There are cigarettes here, and an evening paper somewhere if you care to look for it . . ."

She went up the stair. He heard her moving about, high heels tapping on the polished floor. She sang under her breath, slightly out of tune. He put down his glass and went into her living-room, and ran her telephone to earth at last, beneath a bundle of flowered chintzes, and called Helen to say he would not be home for dinner. Then he went back to pour the third drink of the evening, and loosened his tie, and flopped once more on the sofa.

The whisky had revived him slightly, and beneath its clean cold bite, his tiredness had changed from end-of-the-day fatigue to a pleasant lassitude. The paper protruded from beneath a cushion, and he pulled it out, and then saw that it was not the *Evening Standard*, but *The Stage*.

"Jane."

"Hello!"

"I didn't know you took *The Stage*."

"I don't."

"Well, it's here."

"Is it?" She didn't sound particularly interested. "Dinah Burnett must have left it behind. You know, she's the actress who needs the bulldozer."

He opened it aimlessly. "Wanted. One All Round Girl

115

Dancer." Why does she have to be all round? Why can't she be all square?

Search me.

He turned to the Repertory page. They were doing Shakespeare at Birmingham, a restoration revival at Manchester, and at Brookford, staging the premiere of a new play . . .

Brookford.

The name leapt at him from the page like a bullet. Brookford. He sat up, slapped the paper into shape, and read the whole item.

Brookford Rep's summer season opens this week with the world premiere of *Daisies on the Grass,* a comedy in three acts by local writer Phyllis Jason. This light but well-knit play stars actress Charmian Vaughan in the lead role of Stella. Other parts are supplementary, but John Rigger, Sophie Lambart and Christopher Ferris all help to bring the mirthful suspense to its climax, and Sara Rutherford is charmingly natural as the bride. Tommy Childers' production is fast and furious, and the set, by scenic artist Brian Dare, evoked a spontaneous applause from the enthusiastic first-night audience.

Christopher Ferris.

He laid the paper carefully down, and reached for a cigarette, and lit it. Christopher Ferris. He had forgotten Christopher.

But now, out of a jumble of memories, he heard Emma's voice again, that first day, when he had given her lunch at Marcello's.

Did you know about Christopher? Quite by chance Christopher and I met up again in Paris. And he came this very morning and saw me off at Le Bourget.

116

And he remembered—facing her across the table—being suddenly wise, and knowing the reason for her smile and the bloom of her skin and the brightness of her eyes.

And later, in the draughty studio at Porthkerris, the subject of Christopher had, fleetingly, come up again, sandwiched between other more important items of discussion. *"He'll be at Brookford by now,"* Emma had said. *"In the thick of rehearsals."*

He stood up and went to the foot of the stairs.

"Jane."

"Hello!"

"How nearly ready are you?"

"I'm just doing my face."

"Where's Brookford?"

"In Surrey."

"How long will it take us to get there?"

"Brookford? Oh, about forty-five, fifty minutes."

He glanced at his watch. "If we leave right away, or as near as we can . . . we shouldn't be too late."

Jane appeared at the head of the stairs, with a mirror in one hand and an eyeliner brush in the other.

"Late for what?"

"We're going to the theatre."

"I thought we were going out for dinner."

"Later, perhaps we will. But first we're going to Brookford, to see a well-knit comedy called *Daisies on the Grass* . . ."

"Have you gone out of your mind?"

". . . By local writer Phyllis Jason."

"You have gone out of your mind."

"I'll explain on the way down. Be a darling and hurry."

As they roared down the M.4 Jane said, "You mean that nobody knows about this young man except you."

"Emma didn't tell Ben, because he'd never liked Christopher anyway—Helen says he was jealous of the boy."

"And Emma didn't tell Marcus Bernstein."

"I don't think so."

"But she told you."

"Yes, she told me. She told me that very first day. And why the devil I didn't think of him before I cannot imagine."

"Is she in love with him?"

"I wouldn't know. She's certainly very fond of him."

"Do you think we'll find her at Brookford?"

"If we don't, then I'll bet even money that Christopher Ferris will know where she is." Jane did not reply. After a little, he added, his eyes still fixed on the speeding road, "I'm sorry about this. I promised the subject wasn't to be raised again, and here I am whisking you off to the wilds of darkest Surrey."

"Why," asked Jane, "are you so anxious to find Emma?"

"Because of Marcus. I should like to set Marcus' mind at rest."

"I see."

"Because if Marcus' mind is at rest, then Helen will relax and life will be a great deal more comfortable for all of us."

"Well, that's fair enough . . . Look, I think we should turn off here."

The Brookford Repertory Theatre took some finding. They cruised up and down the High Street, then asked directions from a tired-looking policeman in shirt sleeves. He sent them a half a mile from the centre of town, and, off a back street, up a cul-de-sac, they found the large brick edifice, looking more like a Mission hall than anything else, but the word THEATRE written above the door in neon letters, deadened by the hot evening light.

Outside, by the pavement, were parked a couple of

cars, and alongside them, with their feet in the gutter, sat two small girls playing with a broken perambulator.

There were posters.

WORLD PREMIERE

DAISIES ON THE GRASS

by PHYLLIS JASON

A comedy in THREE ACTS

Produced by

TOMMY CHILDERS

Jane stood, taking in this unauspicious façade. "So much for the living theatre."

Robert put his hand under her elbow . . . "Come along now."

They went up a flight of stone steps, and into a small foyer, with a cigarette kiosk on one side, and a box office on the other. In the box office a girl sat knitting.

"I'm afraid the show's started," she said, as Robert and Jane appeared on the other side of the glass.

"Yes, we thought it would have. But we'll have a couple of tickets anyway."

"What price?"

"Oh . . . well—stalls."

"That's fifteen shillings, please. But you'll have to wait till the second act."

"Is there anywhere we could get a drink?"

"The bar's upstairs."

"Thank you very much." He took the tickets and his change. "I expect you know all the people who work here."

"Well, yes . . ."

"Christopher Ferris . . ."

"Oh, is he a friend of yours?"

"Well, a friend of a friend. The thing is, I wondered if

119

he has his sister here . . . at least, she's his step-sister. Emma Litton."

"Emma's working here."

"She's *working* here. In the theatre?"

"That's right. As A.S.M.—Assistant Stage Manager. Our last girl suddenly went off ill with an appendix, and Emma said she'd come and help out. Of course," her voice became professional . . . "Mr. Childers usually likes someone in the job who's had a bit of stage training, you know, RADA, or a bit of experience somewhere, so that they double up in small parts. But as she was here, and didn't have anything to do, he let her have the job. Just until the regular girl's better."

"I see. Do you think we'd be able to see her?"

"Well, after the show, yes. But Mr. Childers won't have anyone back stage until it's over."

"That's all right. We can wait. Thank you very much."

"Not at all. It's a pleasure."

They went upstairs to a second, larger foyer with a bar in the corner, and sat there, drinking lager and talking to the barman until a light spatter of applause announced the end of the first act. The lights went up, the doors opened, and a small stream of people emerged for refreshment. Jane and Robert waited until the first curtain bell, and then went into the auditorium themselves, buying a couple of programmes on their way, and being shown to their seats by an eager young girl in a nylon overall. Attendance that night was certainly sparse, and Jane and Robert were the only two people sitting in the third row. Jane looked about her with a professional eye.

"I think it was once a mission hall," she decided. "Nobody would have built anything so ugly as a theatre. But I must say, they have done it up quite imaginatively, and the lighting and the colours are good. What a shame they don't get better audiences . . ."

The curtain at last went up on the second act. "The lounge hall of Mrs. Edbury's house in Gloucestershire" said the programme note, and there it was, complete with french windows, staircase, settee, table with drinks, table with telephone, low table with magazines (for leading lady to pick up and idly flick through in moments when she did not know what to do with her hands?) and three doors.

"Draughty house," murmured Jane.

"It's better when they shut the french windows."

But the french window had to be open, for in bounced the ingénue (*Sara Rutherford is charmingly natural as the bride*), flung herself on the settee and burst into tears. Jane's profile was alert with delighted disbelief. Robert settled more deeply into his seat.

It was a terrible play. Even if they had seen the first act, and so been able to unravel the tangled skein of the plot, it would still have been a terrible play. It bristled with clichés, with stock characters (there was even a comic charlady), with contrived exits and entrances, and with telephone calls. There were eight of these in the course of the second act alone.

When the curtain came down, Robert said, "Let's go and have another drink. I could do with a double brandy after that."

"I'm not going to move," said Jane. "I'm not going to break the spell. I haven't seen a play like this since I was seven. And the set makes me positively nostalgic. But there's one thing, Robert, that sticks out like a sore thumb."

"What's that?"

"Christopher Ferris is very, very good . . ."

He was, too. When he had shambled on stage, as the vague young university student who was eventually to win the heroine from her stockbroker fiancé, *Daisies on the Grass* showed its first, faint spark of life. His lines were not better than anyone else's, but his timing was impeccable, and he managed to make them funny or sad, or wryly charming. For the part he wore corduroys, a sagging sweater and horn-rimmed spectacles, but even these could not disguise his elegance and his good looks and the natural long-legged grace with which he moved.

". . . and he's not merely very good, he's very attractive," Jane went on. "I can see why his step-sister was so pleased to bump into him again in Paris. I wouldn't mind bumping into him myself."

The third act had the same set, but now it was night. Blue moonlight shone through the open window, and down the stairs came the little bride, carrying a suitcase, tiptoeing, all ready to run away or elope or whatever it was she'd spent the last hour in deciding to do. Robert couldn't remember. He was waiting for Christopher to come back on stage. When he did, Robert simply watched him the entire time, detachedly, absorbed and full of admiration. By now, he had the audience, small as it was, in the palm of his hand. As Robert watched, so they watched. Christopher scratched the back of his head and they laughed. He took off his spectacles to kiss the girl, and they laughed again. He put them back on to say good-bye for ever, and there was silence, and then people began to blow their noses. And when it was all over, and the cast lined up for the curtain call, the applause was long, and real, and it was all for Christopher.

"What do we do now?" asked Jane.

"It's not closing time for another ten minutes. Let's go and find a drink."

They went back to the bar. The barman said, "Well, how did you enjoy the show, sir?"

"Well, I don't know . . . I . . ."

Jane was braver. "We thought it was terrible," she said, but quite politely. "And I've fallen in love with Christopher Ferris."

The barman grinned. "Quite something, isn't he? Pity you had to come to-night, when the audience was so thin on the ground as it were. Mr. Childers did hope, Miss Jason being local and all that jazz, that this play would bring them in. But you can't fight a heat wave."

"Do you usually have good houses?" Jane wanted to know.

"They go up and down. Now, last show we did was *Present Laughter* . . . that fairly filled the place up."

"It's a good play," said Robert.

"What part did Christopher Ferris have?" asked Jane.

"Now, let me see. Oh, I know, he was the young playwright. You know, the one that bounces round on the chairs and eats biscuits. Ronald Maule he's called in the play. Oh, very funny, Christopher Ferris was in that part. Brought the house down, he did . . ." Wiping away at his tumblers, he glanced up at the clock. "I'm afraid I'll have to ask you to drink up, sir . . . closing time . . ."

"Yes, of course. By the way, how do we get back stage? We want to see Emma Litton."

"You can just go down the auditorium, sir, go through the door at the right of the stage. But watch out for Mr. Collins the Stage Manager. He doesn't exactly relish visitors."

"Thanks," said Robert. "And good-night."

They went back into the theatre. The curtains had been drawn back, and the stage was revealed once more, but without footlights the set looked less inspiring than ever. On stage a young boy was struggling with the sofa, trying to heave it to one side, and someone, somewhere had left a door open, so that the whole theatre was swept with a stuffy draught of used-up air. The programme girl was going round, slapping up the empty seats and collecting empty chocolate boxes and cigarette cartons in a trash can.

"There is nothing," said Jane, "so depressing as an empty theatre."

They started to walk down towards the stage. As they approached, Robert realised that it was not a boy who struggled, single-handed with the heavy sofa, but a girl, dressed in an old blue sweater and jeans.

When he was close enough, he said, "I wonder if you can help me . . . ?"

She turned to look at him, and Robert, with the shock of sheer disbelief, found himself face to face with Emma Litton.

After a second's gaping silence, Emma stopped trying to move the sofa, and straightened up. He thought that she seemed much taller and thinner, the cold stage light was not flattering, her wrists hung like sticks from her rolled-up sleeves. But the worst thing was her hair. She had cut off her hair, and now her head seemed small and vulnerable, furred like the pelt of an animal.

There was the animal feel of watchfulness about her, too. A scarey look as though she waited for him to make the first move, to say the first word, before she knew which way to jump. He slid his hands into his pockets, in a deliberate attempt to both look and feel casual, and he said, "Hello, Emma."

She gave the ghost of a smile. She said, "This sofa feels

as though it's been stuffed with lead and lost its castors in the process."

"Isn't there anyone who can help you?" He came forward to the edge of his side of the stage, so that he was looking up at her. "It looks very heavy."

"Yes, there'll be someone in a moment." She did not seem to know what to do with her hands. She rubbed them on the seat of her jeans as though they were dirty, and then folded her arms. It was a curiously defensive movement, and made her shoulder-bones jut forward beneath the thin cotton of her shirt. "What are you doing here?"

"We came down to see *Daisies in the Grass* . . . We drove down from town. This is Jane Marshall. Jane, this is Emma."

They smiled, nodded at each other, murmured how do you do? Emma turned back to Robert. "Did . . . did you know I was here?"

"No, but I knew Christopher was, and I thought you might be."

"I've been working for a couple of weeks. It gives me something to do."

Robert made no comment on this, and, perhaps disconcerted by his silence, Emma suddenly sat down on the sofa that she was meant to be shifting. Her hands hung listlessly between her knees. After a little, she said, "Did Marcus send you?"

"No. We just came to call. Make sure you're all right . . ."

"I'm all right."

"What time are you finished here . . . ?"

"I'll be about half-an-hour. I have to clear the stage for rehearsal to-morrow morning. Why?"

"I thought we might have all gone to some hotel or

other, for a sandwich and a drink. Jane and I haven't had any dinner . . ."

"Oh, how kind!" She did not sound enthusiastic. "Well . . . the thing is . . . that I usually leave something in the oven at the flat . . . a casserole or something. Johnny and Chris never eat anything otherwise. We'll have to go back or it'll burn."

"Johnny?"

"Johnny Rigger. He was the fiancé. You know, the other man. He lives with Christo . . . and me."

"I see."

There was another silence. Emma, discomfited, struggled with her more hospitable instincts. "I would ask you to come back, if you'd like to, but there's nothing but a few cans of beer . . ."

"We like beer," said Robert promptly.

"And the flat's in a dreadful mess. There never seems to be time to clean it properly. Not now that I'm working, I mean."

"We don't mind. How do we get there?"

"Well . . . have you got a car?"

"Yes. It's outside."

"Yes . . . well. If you go out and wait, Christo and I will join you later. If that's all right. And then we can show you where it is."

"Splendid. How about Johnny?"

"Oh, he'll be along later."

"We'll wait for you."

He took his hands out of his pockets and turned, and he and Jane walked back up the slight slope of the auditorium. As they reached the double doors, and Robert held one half open for Jane to go through, all hell seemed to break loose on stage.

"Where the devil is that Litton girl?" Robert was in time to see Emma scramble off the sofa as though someone had set off a firework, and try once more to move the cumbersome thing. A small man with a black beard shot on stage, looking like the worst-tempered sort of pirate. "Look, ducky, I asked you to move the bloody sofa, not to go to sleep on it. God, I'll be thankful to see that other girl back and you safely out of this place . . ." One either had to go and knock him down, or withdraw. For Emma's sake Robert withdrew.

The door swung shut behind him, but as they crossed the foyer, the voice could still be heard . . . "She's a moron, we all know, but no one could be as crassly stupid as you . . ."

"Charming," said Jane, as they went down the stair. Robert did not reply, because, until the white-hot blaze of anger with which he had been suddenly consumed, died down, he was not capable of saying anything. "That must be Mr. Collins, the stage manager. Not a very nice man to work for."

They reached the street door, and went down the steps and crossed the pavement and got into the car. It was dark now, a soft, bloomy dusk had descended upon the town, but the heat of the day still lingered, held by the narrow confines of the street, by sunbaked stone and paving. Above them the Theatre sign shone brightly, but as they got into the car, someone from inside the building turned it off. The evening's entertainment was over. Robert reached for his cigarettes, gave Jane one and lit it, and then took one for himself. After a moment he felt a little calmer.

He said, "She's cut off all her hair."

"Has she? What was it like before?"

"Long and silky and dark."

"She doesn't want us to go to-night. You know that, don't you?"

"Yes, I know that. But we must. We don't need to stay long."

"And I hate beer."

"I'm sorry. Perhaps someone will make you some coffee."

". . . It isn't even as though it's a job that requires any sort of brain. The most idiotic creature straight out of RADA could do it more competently than you."

Collins was letting fly, unloading the day's tensions and frustrations in a flood of invective that was directed solely at Emma. He hated her. It had something to do with Christopher; with the fact that her father was both successful and famous. At first, she had tried sticking up for herself, but now she knew better than to try and stem this venomous flood. With Collins, you couldn't win. She simply listened, got on with her work, tried not to let him see how deeply he could upset her.

". . . you got this job because I have to have someone to help me . . . God help me. You didn't get it because Christo shoved his oar in, and you didn't get it because some fool is willing to pay twenty thousand for a Ben Litton of red spots on a blue background. I've got more sense than that, as by now you have no doubt found out. So don't start thinking you can loll around entertaining your toffee-nosed friends . . . and the next time they condescend to visit our humble little show, tell them to bloody well wait till we've finished, will you? Now come on, get that sofa out of the bloody way . . ."

It was nearly eleven before at last he let her go, and then she found Christo waiting for her in Tommy Childers' office. The door was open and she heard them talking, and she knocked and put her head in and said, "I'm ready now. I'm sorry I was so long."

Christo stood up. "That's all right." He stubbed out his cigarette. "Good-night, Tommy."

" 'Night, Christo."

"Thanks for everything."

"That's O.K., old chap . . ."

They went downstairs towards the stage door. He put his arm around her as they went. Their warm bodies touched, it was too hot for such contact, but she found it comforting. Outside, in the little alley that led down to the street, he stopped by the dustbins to light another cigarette.

He said, "You were long enough. Collins playing up?"

"He was furious because Robert Morrow's here."

"Robert Morrow?"

"He's in Bernstein's, with Marcus. He's Marcus's brother-in-law. I told you. He came down to see the show . . . He's brought a girl with him."

Christo stood, looking down at her. "To see the show or to see you?"

"I think to see us both."

"He can't try to take you back. Say you're under age or anything?"

"Of course not."

"Then that's all right."

"Yes, I suppose it is. But, you see, like a fool, I asked them back to the flat. At least, I didn't mean to ask them, but somehow I did, and they're coming. They're waiting for us now, in the car. Oh, Christo, I am sorry."

He laughed. "*I* don't mind."

"They won't stay long."

"I don't mind if they stay all night. Don't look so tragic." He took her in his arms, and kissed her cheek. She thought that if only the evening, the day, the endless day, could end right here and now, she would be well content. She was afraid of Robert. She was too tired to fence with him, to answer questions, to try and evade those watchful grey eyes. She was too tired to compete with his friend, who was blonde and pretty and almost indecently cool-looking in her sleeveless navy-blue dress. She was too tired to tidy the flat for them, to shovel clothes and scripts and empty glasses out of sight, to open beer cans, and make coffee, and get Christo's dinner out of the oven.

Christo rubbed his chin against her cheek. "What's wrong?" he asked gently.

"Nothing." He did not like her to say she was tired. He was never tired. He did not know what the word meant.

He said, in her ear, "It's been a good day, hasn't it?"

"Yes, of course." She drew away from him. "A good day." With their arms entwined, they went down the alley towards the street. Robert heard their voices, and got out of the car to meet them. They came towards him, in and out of the patches of light flung by the street lamps. They walked like lovers, Emma trailing a sweater, Christo with a bulky script under one arm and a cigarette between his fingers. When they reached the car, they stopped. "Hello," said Christopher, smiling.

"Christo, this is Robert Morrow, and Miss Marshall . . ."

"Mrs. Marshall," Jane corrected sweetly, leaning over the back of the front seat. "Hello, Christopher."

"Sorry we've been so long," said Christo . . . "Emma's only just told me you were here. And she was having her nightly set-to with Collins, so we've all been fairly occupied. I believe you're coming back to have a can of beer, or something. I'm afraid we've got nothing stronger."

131

"That's O.K.," said Robert. "If you can tell us the way . . ."

"Of course."

The flat was in the basement of a row of daunting Victorian houses that had once seen better days. They were much gabled, and decorated with fancy brick work and stained windows, but the street itself was dismal, and the curtains of bow-windowed front rooms sagged sadly and were not always very clean. Worn stone steps led down to an area where there were dustbins and one or two dead geraniums in pots, and, as they descended, there was a scream of fury from a frustrated cat, and a black, rat-like form shot up the stairs between their legs. Jane let out a small scream of fright.

"It's all right," said Emma. "It's only a cat."

Christo opened the door, and went ahead, turning on cold overhead lights, for the flat was a furnished one, and not supplied with lamps. Johnny had started making a couple out of Chianti bottles but had got no further than buying adaptors and a pair of fancy shades. The rooms of the flat had been sketchily converted, and it was still sadly obvious that their original intentions had been kitchens, larders, and wash-houses. An old range had been torn from the wall, and the resultant void filled with shelves, which no-one had ever bothered to paint, and which acted as a catch-all for books, shoes, scripts, cigarettes, letters and a pile of old magazines. There was a divan which had been covered with an orange curtain and piled with thinly-filled cushions, but remained stubbornly a bed. There were one or two rickety kitchen chairs and a folding table, and the flagged floor was sparsely covered by an elderly carpet which had long since lost all colour and most of its pile. The walls had been whitewashed, but there were oozing damp stains like maps, and the corners of a bull-fighting poster, stuck to the bricks, was already beginning to curl. There was the smell of mice and dry rot, and, even on this hot summer evening, the very airlessness was clammy, like the inside of a cave.

Christo dropped his script on a table and went to open the window which was protected with iron bars, like a prison.

"Let's have some air. We have to keep the place shut up because of the cats, they get in anywhere. What would you like to drink? . . . There is beer, if Johnny hasn't drunk it all . . . or perhaps you'd like coffee. Have we got any coffee, Emma . . . ?"

"There's some instant coffee. I don't get the other sort, because there's nothing to make it in. Do sit down . . . sit on the bed. Sit anywhere. There are some cigarettes . . ." She found them, a box of fifty, handed them round, searched for an ashtray while Robert lit them. There was no ashtray, so she went down the flagged passage to the kitchen for a couple of saucers. The sink was full of dirty dishes, and for a moment she could not think when they had used them, when she had last been here, from what back-log of history they dated. Pinned down, remembered, the morning seemed three weeks away. No day had ever lasted for longer. And now, it was past eleven o'clock at night, and still it was not over. Still, the boys had to be given their supper, the kettle boiled for coffee, the can-opener found.

She found two clean saucers and took them back to the others. Christo had put on a record. He could do nothing, not even talk, without perpetual background music. It was Ella Fitzgerald and Cole Porter.

Every time we say good-bye
I die a little.

133

They were talking about *Daisies on the Grass*. ". . . if you can breathe life into a script like that," Jane was saying to Christopher, ". . . I'm sure you're going to go far." She was laughing. Emma put down the ashtray, and Jane looked up. "Thank you . . . is there anything I can do?"

"No, nothing. I'll just go and get some glasses. Would you like beer, or would you rather have coffee?"

"Would coffee be too much trouble?"

"No, not at all . . . I'd like coffee too . . ."

Back in the kitchen, she closed the door, so that they would not hear her clattering dishes, and tied on an apron, and put a kettle on to boil. When she lit the gas, it always backfired and frightened her out of her wits. She found a tray and cups and saucers, the tin of coffee, sugar, the cans of beer in a box beneath the sink. There were black beetles on the floor and Johnny had not emptied the trash can. She picked it up to take it out to the dustbin, but as she did so the door behind her opened, and she turned to face Robert Morrow.

He looked at the bucket. "Where are you taking that?"

"Nowhere," said Emma, furious at being caught. She turned to sling it back under the sink again, but he caught her arm and took it from her, looking with distaste at the mixture of old tea-leaves and opened tins, and wet paperbags.

"Where does this go?"

Defeated, Emma told him. "In the dustbin. By the door. Where we came in."

He bore it off, down the passage, looking ridiculous, and Emma went back to the sink, and wished that he had not come. He didn't belong in Brookford; at the theatre; here, in the flat. She didn't want him to be sorry for her. For after all, there was nothing to be sorry about. She was happy, wasn't she? She was with Christo, and that was all that mat-

tered, and how they managed their affairs had nothing whatever to do with Robert.

She prayed that he and his immaculate friend would be
gone by the time Johnny Rigger returned.

When he came back with the empty bucket, she was
clattering dishes, trying to give the impression that she was
being busy. She half-turned over her shoulder and said
coolly, "Thank you. I shan't be a moment," hoping that he
would take the hint and leave her alone.

But it was no good. He shut the door, put the trash can
down on the floor, and taking Emma by the shoulders,
turned her round to face him. He wore an unrumpled and
cool-looking suit, a blue shirt, and a dark tie, and Emma had
the dish-mop in one hand and a plate in the other, and had
to make herself look up and meet those probing grey eyes.

She said, "I wish you hadn't come. Why did you
come?"

"Marcus has been worried about you." He took the
dish-mop and the plate from her and leaned over to tip them
back into the cluttered sink. "Perhaps you should have let
him know where you were."

"Well, now you can tell him, can't you? And, Robert,
I've got a lot to do, and there's just not room for two people
in this kitchen . . ."

"Isn't there?" He was smiling. He settled himself on
the edge of the table, and now his face was on a level with
hers. He said, "You know, this evening, when I first saw you
in the theatre I didn't know it was you. Why did you cut
your hair?"

He could be very disarming. Emma put up a hand to
stroke the stubbly nape of her neck. "When I started working at the theatre, it was such a nuisance. It got in the way,
and then it was so hot, and it was always being splashed with
paint when I was doing scenery. And there's nowhere here

135

to wash it, and even if I did wash it, it took hours to dry." She hated talking about her hair. She missed it; missed its weight and familiarity and the soothing therapy of brushing it each night. "So one of the girls in the theatre cut it off for me." It had lain on the Green Room carpet like skeins of brown silk and Emma had felt like a murderer.

"Do you like working in the theatre?"

She thought of Collins. "Not much."

"Do you have to . . . ?"

"No, of course not. But Christo's there all day, you see, and there's nothing much to do here, on my own. Brook-ford's terribly dull. I didn't know such dull places even existed. So when this other girl went ill with appendicitis, Christo fixed it for me to go and help out."

"What will you do when she comes back?"

"I don't know. I haven't thought."

Behind her, the kettle boiled over. Emma turned swiftly to put out the gas, and lift the kettle on to the tray, but Robert said, "Not just yet."

She frowned. "I was going to make coffee."

"Coffee can wait. Let's get everything sorted out first."

Emma's face closed up. "There's nothing to sort out."

"Yes, of course there is. And I want to be able to tell Marcus what happened. For instance, how did you get hold of Christopher?"

"I rang him up—early that Sunday morning. I went to the call box and rang him up. They were having a dress rehearsal, so he was at the theatre. You see, he'd already asked me to come to Brookford and be with him, but I couldn't, because of Ben."

"You'd already spoken to him that morning, when I came to say good-bye?"

"Yes."

"And you never told me?"

"No, I didn't tell you. I wanted to start something quite new, a whole new life, without anybody knowing."

"I see. So you rang Christopher . . ."

"Yes, and that night he borrowed Johnny Rigger's car, and he came down to Porthkerris and brought me back here. We closed up the cottage together, and we left the key of the studio at the Sliding Tackle."

"The landlord didn't know where you were."

"I didn't tell him where I was going."

"Marcus phoned him."

"Marcus shouldn't have. Marcus isn't responsible for me any more. I'm not a little girl now."

"What Marcus feels is not simply responsibility, Emma, but a real fondness and you should realise that. Have you heard from Ben?"

"Yes, I had a letter on that Monday morning, before I left Porthkerris. And one from Melissa, too . . . asking me to go out and visit them."

"And did you write back?"

Emma shook her head. "No." She was ashamed of this, and swiftly looked down, to fiddle with a jagged thumb nail.

"Why not?"

She shrugged. "I don't know. I suppose I thought I'd be in the way."

"I should have thought that even being in the way was preferable to this . . ." His gesture embraced the littered kitchen, the whole seedy flat.

It was not the most fortunate of remarks. "What's wrong with it?"

"It's not just this place, it's that crumby theatre, the lunatic with a beard who was yelling at you to move the sofa . . ."

"Well, you told me to get a job."

"Not this kind of a job. You have a good brain, you

137

speak three languages, and you appear to be moderately intelligent. What sort of a job it is pushing furniture around a
third class re . . . ?"

"My real job is being with Christo!"

After this outburst, there was a terrible silence. A car
passed in the street outside. Christopher's voice came up the
stone passage, backed by the soft-playing record. A cat
started yowling.

Robert spoke at last. "Do you want me to tell your
father that?"

Emma blazed once more into the attack. "I supposed
that's why you came. Spying for Ben."

"I simply came to find out where you were and how
you were."

"Be sure to give him all the ghoulish details. It doesn't
matter to us, and he won't take any notice, anyway."

"Emma . . ."

"Don't forget, he is no ordinary, run-of-the-mill parent,
as you are only too fond of telling me."

"Emma, will you listen . . . !"

The last word was scarcely out of his mouth, when the
door behind him burst open and a slurred and cheerful voice
broke in. "Well, what a nice little chat you two are having!"

Robert wheeled. In the open doorway stood the young
man who had played the part of the stuffy stockbroker in
Daisies on the Grass. Only now he was stuffy no longer, but
quite simply very drunk, and to steady himself hung on to
the top of the doorway, like a monkey swinging on a trapeze.
His legs, buckling slightly, did nothing to dispel this impression.

"Hello, darling," he said to Emma. He let go of the
door and weaved into the tiny kitchen, rendering it unbearably crowded. With the palms of his hands flat on the table,

he leaned forward to kiss Emma. The kiss was loud and smacking, but did not come within six inches of her face.

"We've got callers," he observed. "And a bloody great car parked outside. It adds great tone to the neighbour-hood." His legs buckled again, and for a second his weight was supported solely by his arms. He smiled expansively at Robert. "What's your name?"

"He's called Robert Morrow," said Emma shortly, "and I'll make you some coffee."

"I don't want coffee. I do not want coffee." He raised his fist to the words, and once more his legs let him down. This time Robert caught him, and hauled him upright.

"Thanks, old boy. Very civil of you. Emma, how about a little sustenance? Feed the inner man; you know the routine. I do hope you've asked this nice chap Robert to stay for dinner. There's also a toothsome blonde in the other room, chatting Christopher up to no mean tune. Know anything about her?"

Nobody bothered to answer him. Emma turned back to the cooker, took the lid off the kettle and put it on again. Johnny Rigger stared at her back and then at Robert, apparently waiting for life, with all its confusions, to be explained to him.

Robert could not trust himself to speak. He yearned to pick up this shambling drunk by the scruff of his neck and chuck him somewhere; preferably in the dust-bin, where he had just dumped the unsavoury contents of the trash can. Then he would come back to deal with Emma in the same way, flinging her into the back of his car, driving her to London, to Porthkerris, to Paris—anywhere, away from this terrible basement, from the theatre, from the depressing suburban town.

He stared at her stubborn back view, willing her to turn round and face up to him. But she did not move, and her thin neck, and her shorn head, and the droop of her shoulders, all of which, he knew, should touch on his sympathy, did nothing but infuriate him.

He said, at last, formally, "This is simply a waste of everybody's time. I think Jane and I should go."

Emma accepted this in silence, but Johnny was full of protests. "Oh, you must stay, old chap. Stay and have something to eat . . ."

But Robert had pushed past him and was already halfway down the flagged passage. He found the other two deep in conversation, and quite unaware of any sort of drama. Christopher was saying, "Yes, it's a wonderful play. And what a part! You can build on to it, yet never overload it, never interfere in any way with production . . ."

(And he remembered bitterly the old crack about actors. "Now, let's talk about *you*, my friend. What did *you* think of my performance?")

"I trust you're not discussing *Daisies on the Grass.*"

Christopher looked round. "Good God, no! *Present Laughter.* What's Emma doing?"

"Your friend has just arrived back."

"Johnny? Yes, we just saw him tottering by."

"He's drunk."

"He quite often is. We fill him up with black coffee and shovel him into his bed. He's right as rain in the morning. Most unfair, really."

"Is there any particular reason why he should have to be here with you and Emma?"

Christopher raised his eyebrows. "Every reason." His voice was cool. "It's his flat. He got here first. I was second. Emma made a very cosy third."

There was a pause in the conversation. Jane, sensing the worst sort of conflict, broke tactfully in.

"Robert, it is getting late . . ." She picked up her bag

and her gloves, and got up off the divan. ". . . Perhaps we should be going."

"But you haven't had your coffee. Or beer, or anything. What is Emma doing?"

"Doing her best to prop up Mr. Rigger," Robert told him. "I suggest you go and help her. His legs don't seem to be at their most reliable."

Christopher, shrugging, acknowledged this. He uncurled his length from the low chair in which he had been sitting, and stood up. "Well, if you really feel you have to go . . ."

"I think we should. Thank you for . . ."

The words died out. There was nothing to thank him for. Christopher looked amused and Jane once again came to Robert's rescue.

". . . thank you for your wonderful performance this evening. We won't forget it." She held out her hand. "Good-bye."

"Good-bye. And good-bye, Robert."

"Good-bye, Christopher." And then he had to make himself say it. "Look after Emma."

They drove with unlawful speed back to London. On the motorway the needle of the speedometer crept up and up. Eighty, ninety, a hundred . . .

Jane said, "You're going to get into trouble."

"I already am," said Robert shortly.

"Did you have a row with Emma?"

"Yes."

"I thought you were looking a little fraught. What was it about?"

"Snooping. And moralising. And interfering. And trying to make a basically intelligent girl see the smallest glimmer of sense. She looked awful, too. She looked ill."

"She'll be all right."

"Last time I saw her, she was brown as a Gipsy, with hair to her waist and a sort of bloom about her, like a delicious ripe fruit." He remembered the pleasure of kissing her good-bye. "Why do people have to do such dreadful things to themselves?"

"I don't know," said Jane. "Perhaps because of Christopher."

"How did you get on with him? I mean, apart from falling in love with him."

She ignored this. "He is clever. He is single-minded. He is ambitious. I think he will go far. But alone."

"You mean, without Emma."

"I'd say that."

Even at one in the morning London was alive with lights and traffic. They turned down into Sloane Street, circled Sloane Square, took the narrow road that led to Jane's mews. Outside her little house, he killed the engine of the Alvis, and it was very quiet. Street lamps shone on to the cobbles, on to the gleaming bonnet of the car, on to Jane's blonde and shining head. Robert was suddenly very tired. He began to reach for a cigarette, but Jane was there first. She put the cigarette into his mouth and lit it for him. In that instant her eyes became large and mysteriously shadowed, and there was a small and beguiling shadow, like a smudge, below the curve of her lower lip.

She snapped out the lighter. He said, "It's been a bloody awful evening. And I'm sorry."

"It always makes a change. It was interesting."

He pulled off his cap and dropped it onto the back seat. "Do you suppose," he said, "that they're living together?"

"Darling, I wouldn't know."

"But she's in love with him."

"I would say so."

For a little they were silent. Then Robert stretched,

flexing himself after the long drive. He said, "We never got any dinner, did we? I don't know about you, but I'm hungry."

"If you want, I'll cook you scrambled eggs. And pour you a big cold Scotch-on-the-rocks."

"You're twisting my arm . . ."

They laughed, quietly. Night time laughter, he thought. Pillow laughter. He put his left hand up and around her neck, slid his fingers up into her hair, and leaned forward to kiss her mouth. She tasted sweet and fresh and cool. Her lips parted, and he threw his cigarette away, and pulled her tightly and closely into his arms.

After a little, he took his mouth from hers. "What are we waiting for, Jane?"

"One thing."

He smiled. "What's that?"

"Me. I don't want to start something that isn't ever going to be finished. I don't want to be hurt again. Even for you, Robert, and God knows how fond I am of you."

He said, "I won't hurt you," and meant it, and kissed the shadow under her mouth.

"And please," she said, "no more Littons."

He kissed her eyes, and the end of her short nose. "It's a promise. No more Littons."

He let her go then, and they got out of the car, and closed the doors as quietly as they had laughed together. And Jane found her key, and Robert took it from her and opened the door, and they went in, and Jane turned on the light, and started up the narrow stair, and Robert closed the door, gently, behind them.

9

One of the delights of the big old house in Milton Gardens was living there in the summer. At the end of a warm and stuffy June day, and after the frustrations of a snail's-pace, petrol-laden journey back down the Kensington High Street, it was a positive physical pleasure to come in through the front door and slam it with happy finality behind you. The house always felt cool. It smelt of flowers and wax-polish, and in June the chestnut trees were out and so thick with leaves and pink and white blossom that the surrounding terraces of houses were shrouded from sight, sounds of all traffic were muffled, and only the occasional aeroplane, passing overhead, broke the evening calm.

To-day was a classic example of this particular relief. There was thunder about, and since morning the temperature had steadily risen as the storm clouds gathered. Beneath this doom-like atmosphere, the city sweltered. By now the parks were dusty and the trampled grass turning brown, and the air about as refreshing as a draught of used bath-water. But here, at home, Helen had the sprinklers working on the lawn, and a gust of sweet, damp air swept through the open door at the end of the hall, and greeted Robert as he came indoors.

He dropped his hat on the hall chair, picked up his letters, called "Helen?"

She wasn't in the kitchen. He went down the hall and out of the door and down the steps to the terrace and found her there, with a tea-tray and a book—unread—and a basket of mending. She wore a sleeveless cotton dress and a faded pair of espadrilles, and the sun had brought freckles out, big as paint spots, across her nose.

He came across the grass towards her, shedding the jacket of his suit.

She said, "You have caught me, doing nothing."

"And very nice too." He slung the jacket over the back of a painted wrought-iron chair, and collapsed beside her. "What a day! Anything left in that teapot?"

"No, but I can make you some more."

"Why don't I?" said Robert automatically, but without notable enthusiasm.

She did not reply to this hypothetical question, simply got up and took the teapot indoors. There was a plate of biscuits, and he took one and began to eat it, pulling his tie loose with the other hand. Beneath the sprinklers the lawn lay thick and green. It needed cutting again. He leaned back and shut his eyes.

It was now six weeks since he had been to Brookford to find Emma Litton, and in all that time there had been no word from her. After some discussion with Marcus and Helen he had written to Ben, telling him that Emma was staying with Christopher Ferris, whom she had re-met in Paris. That she was working in the Repertory Theatre in Brookford. That she was well. He could not, in truth, say more. Surprisingly, Ben had acknowledged this, not directly, to Robert, but as a scribbled footnote to a letter to Marcus. The purpose of the letter itself was purely business, type-written on the impressive engraved paper of the Ryan Memorial Museum of Fine Arts. The retrospective Litton Exhibition was now over. In every way it had been a resounding success. Now, the new exhibition—a posthumous collection of drawings of a Puerto Rican genius who had lately died in dismal circumstances in a Greenwich Village garret, was well under way, and he and Melissa were taking the opportunity of a trip to Mexico. He intended to start painting again. He did not know when he would be returning to London. He remained, always, Marcus' Ben. And then, under the signature, and in Ben's own indecipherable scrawl:

"Had a letter from R. Morrow. Please thank him. Emma always fond of Christopher. Only hope his manners have improved."

Marcus showed this to Robert. "I don't know what you expected," he said, dryly, "but this is what you have got."

So it was over. For the first time Robert found himself in whole-hearted agreement with his sister Helen. The Littons were brilliant, unpredictable and charming. But they refused to conform to any pre-set behaviour pattern and they would not help themselves. So they were impossible.

To his surprise, he found that Emma was easy to forget. He could put her out of his mind as ruthlessly as an old trunkful of junk, relegated to the darkest recesses of some distant, dusty attic. And his life immediately became so full that the void left by her going was, almost at once, filled by more worthwhile pursuits.

At the Gallery, they were furiously busy. His days were a round of prospective clients, foreign visitors, and eager young artists carrying folios which bulged with their unsalubrious paintings. Would Bernstein mount an exhibition for them? Would Bernstein back this flame of new talent? The answer was usually, No, Bernstein's would not, but Marcus was a kindly man, and it was a house rule that no young man was returned to Glasgow or Bristol or Newcastle, or wherever it was he lived, without a good meal in his stomach, and the price of his return fare in the pocket of genuinely work-stained jeans.

Robert found that his vitality leapt to meet these demands, and, running at full speed, his energy could not—or would not—slow down. He could not bear to find himself doing nothing, and deliberately filled his leisure time with extraneous diversions, and a surprising number of them were involved with Jane Marshall.

The fact that their working hours did not always coincide put him off not at all. Sometimes he would call in for a drink at her little house, on the way home from the Gallery, and find her still in an apron, sewing braid onto yards of curtain, or working out the intricacies of a scallopped pelmet on graph paper. Sometimes she was out of town, and then he would fill the evening with furious physical labour, digging the garden or mowing the lawn.

One week-end he and Jane went down to Bosham, where Jane's brother had a small cottage, and kept a catamaran moored out on the choppy waters of the Hard. They sailed all Sunday and there was a stiff breeze and a bright, burning sun, and at the end of the day, sleepy with all the fresh air, they sat in the village pub and drank draught bitter and played shove ha'penny, and drove back to London very late, with the roof of the Alvis down, and wind blowing scraps of cloud across the face of the stars.

Once more Helen started saying, "I think you should marry her."

Robert ignored the nudging suspicion that he was behaving badly, and only said, "Perhaps I will."

"But when? What are you waiting for?"

He did not answer because he did not know. He only knew that this was not the time to plan; or assess; or to start to analyse the feelings that he had for Jane.

Now, he was disturbed, by Helen, returning with his tea-tray. She set it down, and the iron table grated on the pavings as she pulled it towards him. She said, "Marcus phoned at lunch-time."

Marcus had had to return to Scotland. The whisky-loving Scottish baronet, who had been so anxious to part with his art treasures, was being baulked by his son, who would presumably inherit the heirlooms and did not want them sold out of hand. Or, if they were to be sold, he wanted three times as much for them as his thirsty father was prepared to ask. After a great deal of expensive telephoning, Marcus had reluctantly decided that another visit must be paid north of the border. Business must always come before personal comforts and preferences, and if, to lay his hands on those pictures, he had to sleep in damp beds and icy rooms and eat appallingly-cooked food, then he was ready to do so.

"How is he getting on?"

"He was reserved. No doubt speaking from some soaring baronial hall, with the old Laird listening from one end of the room, and the young Laird listening from the other."

"Has he got the pictures?"

"No, but he will. If not all, then some of them . . ."

She went away from him, across the grass, to move the

sprinkler. "The Raeburn he is determined on," she said, over her shoulder. "He'll go to any price."

Robert poured his tea, and began to read the evening paper. When Helen came back, he handed it to her open at a middle page.

"What's this?" she asked.

"That girl. Dinah Burnett . . ."

"Who is she?"

"You should know her face by now. She's a young actress with an efficient publicity agent. Every time you open a paper or a magazine, there's a picture of her perched on a piano, or cuddling a kitten or something equally obnoxious."

Helen made a comic face at the thrusting, sexy photograph, and read the caption aloud.

Dinah Burnett, the red-head who made such an impact on the TV series *Detective*, is in rehearsal now for the new Amos Monihan play *The Glass Door*, her first serious stake in legitimate theatre. "I'm scared," she told our special reporter. "But so very proud to have been chosen for this wonderful play." Miss Burnett is twenty-two and comes from Barnsley.

"I didn't know there was a new Amos Monihan play on the stocks. Who's producing?"

"Mayo Thomas."

"Then she must be good. Extraordinary, what talent can lurk behind really very stupid faces. But why did you suddenly show this to me?"

"No reason, really. Just that Jane's doing up a flat for her. At first it was going to be a pretty modest affair, but as soon as she got this part, she reckoned she'd moved in with the big-time spenders; you know, mirror bathrooms and white mink bedcovers."

149

"Very nice," said Helen. She tossed the paper back into his lap but he was too hot and lazy to catch it, so it slipped from his knee and fell to the ground. After a little, Helen began, in a desultory fashion, to gather the tea things together. She picked up the tray and started indoors.

"How about dinner?" she asked. "You going to Jane's or are you staying here?"

"I'm going to Jane's."

"That's fine. I'll eat a piece of cheese. It's too hot to cook, anyway."

When she had gone, he lit a cigarette and sat, listening to the pigeons, and watching the shadows lengthen over the grass. The cool and the quiet were like a benediction. The cigarette finished, he got up and went back into the house, and upstairs to his own flat, where he showered and shaved, and changed into jeans and a cool shirt. As he was pouring the first drink of the evening, the telephone rang. He filled the tumbler halfway up with soda, and went to his desk to answer it. It was Jane.

"Robert?"

"Yes."

"Darling, it's me. Look, I just wanted to warn you, don't get here till about eight . . ."

"Why, are you entertaining a lover?"

"Wish I were. No, it's Dinah Burnett, she's had a new idea for her bathroom, God rot her soul, and she wants to come along after rehearsals and talk about it."

"For a girl who is so proud about being in the blasted play, her mind does harp on material things, doesn't it?"

"So you've been reading the evening paper. That blurb makes me ill."

"I can't think why she didn't bother to mention that she was doing up a flat, and had chosen well-known interior decorator, twenty-seven-year-old Jane Marshall, 34, 26, 36, to help her. Were you expecting to be taken out for dinner, because I'm not dressed according."

"Of course not, it's much too hot. I've got some cold chicken; I thought I'd make a salad."

"And I shall subscribe a frosty bottle of wine."

"Delicious."

"Till eight, then."

"Yes, eight." He was on the point of putting down the receiver when she said again, "Don't come before," and than rang off. Mildly puzzled, he put down the receiver and then decided that he must have imagined a certain urgency in her voice. He went to find ice for his drink.

Deliberately, he was a little late, but even so, when he drew up outside Jane's house, there was a small blue Fiat still parked by her door. He gave his double toot on the horn and got out of the car, carrying the bottle of wine, and almost at once the front door opened and Jane stood there, in a faded pair of pink cotton trousers and a sleeveless top. Her hair fell across her cheek and she looked, for Jane, mildly distraught, making flapping gestures with her hand, and pointing upstairs.

He was amused. He came to kiss her. "What is it?"

She took the bottle of wine from him. "She's still here. She won't go. She won't stop talking. And now you've come, nothing's going to shift her."

"We'll say we're going out, and that we're late already."

"I suppose it's worth a try." They had been talking in whispers. Now she said in clear and social tones, "I wasn't sure if it was you or not. Come along up."

He followed her up the narrow, steep stair. "Dinah, this is Robert Morrow . . ." Casually she introduced them, before going into the kitchen with the wine. He heard the big fridge door open and shut as she put it away.

Dinah Burnett sat on Jane's big sofa by the open window, with her legs curled up beneath her, looking as though she was expecting a photographer, or an interviewer, or a prospective lover. She was a beautiful girl, ripe and colourful, and it occurred to Robert that no photograph could do her full justice. She had auburn hair and pale green eyes, and skin like an apricot, and was built on proportions that are normally described as "lavish." She wore a short shift dress in a green to match her eyes, and it might have been designed to display as much as possible of her smooth, well-rounded arms and endless legs. Her feet were thrust into wooden sandals, her wrists jangled with gold bracelets and in her ears, gleaming through the profusion of hair, were enormous gold hoop earrings. Her teeth were white and even, and her black lashes long and black as soot, and it was hard to believe that she had started life in Barnsley.

"How do you do," said Robert. They shook hands. "I've just been reading all about you in the evening paper."

"Wasn't it a dreadful photograph?" She still had an endearing trace of a Yorkshire accent. "I look like a broken-down barmaid. But still, I suppose it's better than nothing."

She smiled at him, all her feminine charm rising to the bait of a new and attractive man, and Robert flattered and warmed by her friendliness, settled himself at the other end of the sofa. She went on, "I shouldn't really be here at all, but Jane's doing up this new flat for me, and to-day I found this American magazine with a fabulous bathroom and I just had to bring it along, after rehearsals, and show it to her."

"How's the play going?"

"Oh, it's most exciting."

"What's it about?"

"Well, it's . . ."

At this juncture Jane re-appeared from the kitchen and briskly interrupted. "How about a drink? Dinah, Robert and

I are actually going out, but there's just time for a drink before you go."

"Oh, that's sweet of you. If you're sure. I'd love a glass of beer."

"How about you, Robert?"

"Sounds very nice, let me get it . . ."

"No, that's all right. I'm up." She snapped the top off a beer bottle, and poured a glass expertly, with no head to it. "Dinah, Robert's an art dealer, he works in Bernstein's in Kent Street."

"Oh, are you really?" said Miss Burnett, looking wide-eyed and interested, but not very much wiser. "Do you sell pictures and stuff. . . . ?"

"Well, yes . . ."

Jane brought Dinah's beer across, pulled up a small table and set the glass down.

"Robert is a very high-powered man," she said. "He's always dashing off to Paris or Rome, to pull off enormous deals, aren't you, Robert?" She went back to her drink tray. "Dinah, you should get him to look out for a picture for the new flat. You need something modern over that fireplace and you never know, it might be an investment. Something to sell when they run out of good parts for you."

"Don't talk about running out. I've only just started. Besides, wouldn't it be very expensive?"

"Not as expensive as that American bathroom."

Dinah smiled engagingly. "But, I always feel a bathroom's terribly important."

Jane had poured two more drinks, now she brought them over, and handed one to Robert. Then settled herself in the chair opposite the sofa, and faced them both across the low table.

"Well, it's your flat, ducky," she said.

Her voice was a little acid. Robert said quickly, "You

still haven't told me about the new play . . . *The Glass Door*. When are you opening?"

"Wednesday. This Wednesday as ever is. At the Regent Theatre."

"We must try and get seats, Jane."

"Yes, of course," said Jane.

"The thought of a first night makes me sick with nerves. You see, it's my first shot at the living theatre, as it were, and if it wasn't for Mayo being such a fabulous producer I'd have dropped out weeks ago. . . ."

"You still haven't told us what it's about."

"Well, it's . . . oh, I don't know. It's about this young man, from an ordinary, working-class family. And he writes a book and it's a best seller, and he becomes a sort of celebrity —you know, on television and such. And then he gets mixed up with the film people, and all the time, he's getting richer, and nastier, and he's drinking and having affairs, and generally living it up. And then, of course, in the end, the whole racket falls round his ears like a pack of cards and he finishes up, right where he started, in his mother's house, in the kitchen, with his old typewriter and a blank sheet of paper. It sounds corny, I know, but it's moving and real and the dialogue is out of this world."

"Do you think it's going to go?"

"I don't see how it can fail. But then I'm prejudiced."

"What part do you play?"

"Oh, I'm just one of the many girls. But I'm different, because I get pregnant."

"Charming," murmured Jane.

"But it isn't sordid, not a bit," Dinah assured her. "When I first read the script I didn't know whether to laugh or cry. Real life, I suppose."

"Yes." Jane finished her drink, and put down the empty glass and looked at her watch. She said, pointedly, "Robert,

I'm going up to change. We mustn't be late. We'll keep everybody waiting." She stood up. "You'll excuse me, Dinah,
won't you?"

"Of course I will, and thank you for being so sweet
about the bathroom. I'll ring you up and let you know what
I've decided."

"Yes, you do that."

When she had gone upstairs, Dinah smiled once more,
confidingly, at Robert. "I hope I'm not keeping you. I will go
when I've finished my drink, but I live in such a dump just
now, it's depressing. And it's so hot, isn't it? I wish it would
thunder. It would be so much cooler if only it would thunder."

"It will this evening, I'm sure. Tell me, how did you get
this part?"

"Well, Amos Monihan, you know, he wrote the play—
he'd seen me on TV in *Detective,* and he rang Mayo Thomas
and said he thought I'd be right for the part. So I had an
audition. That's all really."

"And who plays the lead? The young man. The writer?"

"This is the gamble. The backers wanted a big name,
somebody famous. But Mayo had found this new boy—he'd
seen him in some provincial rep, and somehow, he convinced the man with the money to give him a try."

"So you have an unknown in the lead?"

"That's about it," said Dinah. "But, believe me, he's
good."

She finished her drink. Upstairs Jane was moving about
in her bedroom, going to and fro, opening and shutting
drawers. Robert got up to retrieve the empty glass. "Would
you like the other half?"

"No, really, I won't. I mustn't keep you any
longer . . ." She stood up, pulling down her dress, and toss-

ing her long hair away from her neck. She called up the stair. "I'm off. Good-bye, Jane!"

"Oh, good-bye." Jane sounded more friendly now that her visitor was actually on her way out.

Dinah started downstairs, and Robert followed her, intending to politely see her off the premises. Over her bright head, he leaned forward to unsnib the latch of Jane's front door. Outside, the mews slumbered in the hot airless evening.

He said, "I'll keep my fingers crossed for Wednesday."

"Bless you."

They went out into the street. He opened the door of the Fiat for her. He said, "What's he called, this young actor?"

Dinah slid into the driving-seat, revealing more leg than was good for anybody's blood pressure.

She said, "Christopher Ferris."

He thought, *So that's why Jane didn't want me to meet you.*

"Christopher Ferris? I know him."

"Do you? How funny."

"At least . . . I knew his sister."

"I don't know anything about his family."

"He's never mentioned her? Emma?"

"Never a word. But then, chaps don't usually talk about their sisters, do they?"

She laughed, and slammed the car door shut, but the window was down, and Robert leaned his elbow on it, like a salesman with a foot in the door.

He said, "I'd like to wish him luck."

"I'll give him a message for you to-morrow."

"Could I ring him up?"

"Well, I suppose you could, but calls aren't exactly wel-

come when we're working." And then she had a bright idea.
"Tell you what, I've got his home number somewhere. I had
to ring up for Mayo, once, and leave a message."

She picked her bag off the other seat, and started to
delve. She brought out a script, a purse, a scarf, a bottle of
sun oil, a diary. She leafed through the diary. "Here it is,
Flaxman 8881. Do you want me to write it down for you?"

"No. I'll remember."

"He might be there now . . . I don't know what he
does in his spare time." She smiled again. "Fancy you knowing him. It's a small world, isn't it?"

"Yes. It's a small world."

She started up her engine. "Well, it's been fun meeting
you. Cheerio."

He stood back. "Goodbye."

The little car roared away down the mews, and he
watched it go. At the junction at the end of the narrow street
it paused for a moment, then shot away, turned left and was
gone, the sound of its engine swallowed into the anonymous
grumble that was London traffic.

He went back into the house, closed the door, went
upstairs. There was no sound from the bedroom.

"Jane."

She began immediately to move about, as though occupied.

"Jane."

"What is it?"

"Come here."

"But I'm not . . ."

"Come down here."

After a moment, she appeared at the head of the stairs,
wrapped in a thin dressing-gown. "What is it?"

"It's Christopher Ferris," said Robert.

She stared down at him, her expression closed and suddenly implacable.

"What about him?"

"You knew he was in this play. That he's been in London all this time."

She came down the stairs toward him. When her face was on a level with his, she said coolly, "Yes, I knew."

"But you never told me. Why not?"

"Perhaps because I don't believe in stirring up muddy ponds. Besides, you promised. No more Littons."

"This has nothing to do with that promise."

"Then what are you getting so hot and bothered about? Look, Robert, I think I feel about this business much the same way as your sister Helen. Bernstein's act, in a professional capacity, for Ben Litton, and after that, their commitments to the family should end. I know about Emma and the sort of life she's led and I'm sorry for her. I went to Brookford with you, and I saw that creepy little theatre and that dreadful flat. But she is adult, and, as you said yourself, highly intelligent . . . What if Christopher is in London? That doesn't mean Emma has been abandoned. It's all part of his job, and she'll accept it as such, I'm sure."

"That still doesn't explain why you never told me."

"Perhaps because I knew all along that you'd start running round in circles like a demented sheepdog. Imagining the worst, nagged by responsibility, simply because the wretched girl is Ben Litton's daughter. Robert, you *saw* her. She doesn't want to be helped. And if you try, you'll just be interfering . . ."

He said slowly, "I don't know if you're trying to convince me, or yourself."

"You fool, I'm trying to make you see the truth."

"The truth is that, as far as we know, Emma Litton is alone, living in a damp basement with a paralytic drunk."

"Isn't that what she chose to do?"

She flung the question at him, and then, before he could reply, pushed past him and went to the trolley and began fiddling about with empty glasses and beer-bottle tops in a feeble pretence at tidying up. He watched, with a great sadness, her back view, the smooth bell of hair, the tiny waist, the small, capable hands. She was unrelenting.

He said gently, "Dinah Burnett gave me Christopher's number. Perhaps it would be better if I rang him from here."

"Do whatever you like." She carried the glasses through to the kitchen. Robert picked up her phone and dialled the remembered number. Jane came back to collect up the empty bottles.

"Hello." It was Christopher.

"Christopher, this is Robert Morrow speaking. You remember, I came down to Brookford . . ."

"To see Emma. Yes, of course. How splendid! How did you know where to find me?"

"Dinah Burnett gave me your number. She also told me about *The Glass Door*. Congratulations."

"You can save them till we see what the critics have to say."

"Still, it's a great effort. Look, I was wondering about Emma."

Christopher's voice turned cautious. "Yes?"

Jane had come back from the kitchen and now stood by the window, her arms folded, looking down into the street.

"Where is she?"

"In Brookford."

"In the flat. With your friend?"

"My friend? Oh, Johnny Rigger? No, he left. He came to rehearsals drunk one morning and the producer slung him out. Emma's on her own."

Carefully controlling his temper, Robert said, "You never thought of ringing up Marcus Bernstein or myself and telling us this?"

"Well, I would have, but before I left Brookford, Emma made me promise not to. So, you see, I couldn't." While Robert, in seething silence, tried to accept this excuse, Christopher went on, sounding suddenly much younger and not so sure of himself. "I tell you what I did do, though. I felt a bit of a heel leaving her like that . . . so I wrote to Ben."

"You wrote to *who*?"

"Her father."

"But what the hell could he do? He's in America . . . he's in Mexico . . ."

"I didn't know he was in Mexico, but I wrote to him care of Bernstein's, and put please forward on the envelope. You see, I felt *someone* should know what had happened."

"And Emma? Is she still working in the theatre?"

"She was when I left. You see, there was really no point her coming up to London with me. I rehearse dawn to dusk as it is, and we'd never have seen each other. Besides, if *The Glass Door* folds up after a week, then I'll need my old Brookford job back again. Tommy Childers is very kindly keeping it open for me. So we decided it would be better if Emma stayed down there."

"And if *The Glass Door* runs for two years?"

"I don't know what would happen then. But right now, I'll be honest with you, things are a bit tricky. This house I'm living in—it belongs to my mother. I'm living with my mother. You can see, what with things being the way they are, it is a bit tricky."

"Yes," said Robert. "Yes, I can see . . . as you say, it's tricky."

* * *

He put down the receiver. Jane, not turning from the window, said, "What's so tricky?"

"He's living with Hester, his mother. And she's obviously refusing to let a Litton darken her door. Silly old bitch. And the drunk flatmate has had the sack, so Emma's on her own. And, to ease his conscience, Christopher has written to Ben Litton to tell him what has happened. And I should like to tie the lot of them together with one great big millstone, and consign them all to a bottomless lake."

"I knew this would happen," said Jane. She turned, then, to face him, her arms still rigidly folded, and he saw that she was not only angry, but deeply upset. "It could be good, this thing between us . . . you know that, don't you, as well as I do. And that's why I didn't tell you about Christopher, because I knew, that if you knew, it would be the end of everything."

He wished he could say *It doesn't have to be the end*, but it was impossible.

"In a way, Robert, all this time, you did keep your promise. You never mentioned Emma. But she was never out of the back of your mind."

Now that it was said, and out in the open, he saw that this was true. He said, hopelessly, "Only because in some extraordinary way, I am involved with her."

"If you are involved with her, it's because you want to be. And it's not good enough, Robert. Not for me. I won't settle for second best. I'd rather go without. I hoped I'd made that clear. With me, it has to be all or nothing at all. I can't go through it all again."

He understood. But could only say that he was sorry.

"I think . . . perhaps, you'd better go."

Her arms were still folded, a barrier against him. There was no way to say goodbye. He could not kiss her. He could not lightly say, "It's been fun" in the best traditions of drawing-room comedy. And he could never forgive her for trying to keep him from Emma.

He said, "I'll go now."

"Yes, do that." But as he started downstairs, she remembered something. "You left the wine."

"Forget about the wine," said Robert.

10

The song was over. The lights were dimmed. Charmian as Oberon moved forward for her final speech. The taped Mendelssohn music—for the meagre proportions of the Brookford Rep did not allow space for an orchestra—stole out across the dark cave of the auditorium and evoked for Emma, sitting at the prompt desk—all the distilled magic of a summer night.

> *Now until the break of day*
> *Through this house each fairy stray . . .*

It was the end of the first week of *A Midsummer Night's Dream*. The financial fiasco of *Daisies on the Grass* had driven the management to a production of Shakespeare which, although it entailed double the work for everybody, ensured an Arts Council grant and full houses, composed mostly of school children and students.

By now Emma was no longer working for Collins, the stage manager. There was a new A.S.M., a young girl fresh from drama school, dedicated, tough and seemingly immune to Collins' barbed tongue. She was on-stage now, in the grey velvet tunic and silvered wings of Cobweb, the fairy, for the huge cast of *The Dream* demanded that every member of the company should be called in and given a part.

Because of this, Tommy Childers had asked Emma to come back and lend a hand with the back-stage activities. During the past fortnight she had coped with a number of jobs; helping in the wardrobe, working in the scenery store; typing scripts, and all the time nipping out for sandwiches and cigarettes, and making endless pots of tea.

To-night, she had been given the job of prompter, and had spent the evening with her eyes glued to the prompt copy, terrified of losing her place, of missing a cue, of letting somebody down. But now, as the play drew to its close, and, knowing the rest of it by heart, she allowed her concentration to relax a little, and indulged in the luxury of watching the stage.

Charmian wore a crown of emerald leaves, a silver tabard and silver tights on her long, slim legs. The audience, caught by the old magic of the words, stayed breathless, spellbound.

> *Trip away; make no stay;*
> *Meet me all by break of day.*

To eke out the cramped wing space on either side of the stage, Tommy Childers had had built a ramp which led down from the stage and into the centre aisle of the auditorium. Now Oberon and Titania, hand-in-hand, and followed by a retinue of fairies, made their exit down this ramp, running, with the draperies flying like exuberant wings, off the lighted stage, and down into the darkness; swift and quiet; up the aisle and out of the double doors at the back with such an airy suddenness that they were gone almost without a sound, without a trace.

And then it was left to Sara Rutherford, playing Puck, as a tilt-eared teenager, with the stage to herself and a single spotlight.

> *If we the shadows have offended,*
> *Think but this, and all is mended.*

She had a little pipe. When she got to "So good night unto you all," she played on it the single thread of notes that was the theme of the Mendelssohn music.

Then, triumphant, "Give me your hands, if we be friends, and Robin shall restore amends." And darkness, and curtain, and applause.

All over. Emma let out a sigh of relief that nothing had gone wrong, shut the prompt copy and sat back in her chair. The cast were surging back on stage for the first curtain call. As he went past her, the boy who played Nick Bottom leant over to whisper,

"Tommy asked me to tell you—there's some chap waiting to see you. He's been sitting in the Green Room for half-an-hour, but Tommy's put him in his office. Thought it might be a bit more private for you. Better go and see what it's all about."

"To see me? But who is it?"

But Bottom was already on stage. The curtain swept up, there was a fresh burst of applause, and smiles and bows and curtseys . . .

Emma's first thought was that it was Christo. But if it

was Christo, why hadn't he said? She went down the wooden steps and along the cat-walk that led to the landing at the head of the stage door stairs. Ahead, down a short passage, the Green Room door stood ajar, showing a glimpse of sagging velvet sofa, the old playbills framed on the walls. Tommy Childers' office led off this passage. The door was shut.

Behind her, the applause died down, and then rose again for the second curtain call.

She opened the door.

It was a tiny room, scarcely bigger than a cupboard; scarcely big enough to contain the desk, and a couple of chairs and a filing cabinet. He sat behind the desk, in Tommy's chair, behind Tommy's personal and private chaos of scripts and letters and programme proofs and production notes. The wall behind him was thumb-tacked with stage photographs. Someone had made him a cup of tea, but he had not deigned to drink it, and it stood before him, horribly cold, untouched. He wore pearly-grey trousers, a russet corduroy jacket, a dark blue cotton shirt and a chrome yellow tie, loosely tied, so that his top button showed. He was browner than ever, and he looked about ten years younger, and almost indecently attractive.

He was smoking an American king-size cigarette, and an ash-tray full of butts was indicative of the length of time he had been waiting for Emma. When she came through the door, he turned his head to look at her, resting his elbow on the desk, his chin on his thumb. His eyes, through the veil of cigarette smoke, remained dark and shadowed and quite unreadable.

He said, sounding mildly irritated, "What have you been doing?" and Emma was too stunned to do anything but tell him.

"Prompting."

"Well, come along in and shut the door."

She did as she was told. The applause from the auditorium was closed away. She found that her heart was thudding, but whether this was due to shock, or pleasure, or a certain apprehension it was impossible to know. She said at last, feebly, "I thought you were in America."

"I was, this morning. Flew back to-day. And yesterday . . . at least I suppose it was yesterday, these International date lines and clocks being changed complicate life to an alarming degree . . . I was in Mexico. Yes; yesterday. Acapulco."

Emma felt for a chair, lowered herself gently on to it before her legs gave way.

"Acapulco?"

"Do you know that the aeroplanes that fly to Acapulco are all painted different colours? And as you go south, the air hostesses do a sort of uniform strip tease. Fascinating." He continued to survey her. "Emma, there's something different about you. That's it, you've cut your hair. What a good idea! Turn around and let me see the back." She did so, swiveling her head cautiously, and watching him out of the corner of her eye. "Much better. Never knew you had such a good shape to your head. Have a cigarette."

He pushed the packet across the desk. Emma took one, and he lit it for her, leaning forward, cupping the flame with his familiar and beautiful hands. As he shook out the match he said, casually, "A great many letters have been winging their way across the Atlantic. None of them written by you."

It was a rebuke. "No. I know."

"Difficult to understand. Not that I minded in particular—though I must say, as it was about the first letter I'd ever written you, it would have been pleasant to get a reply. But with Melissa it was different. She wanted you to come out to the States, and be with us, if only for a short visit.

167

You've always been rather good about these things. What happened?"

"I don't know. I suppose I was . . . disappointed because you didn't come home. And the idea of your being married took a bit of time to get used to. And then, by the time I got round to accepting it . . . it had become too late to answer your letters. And every day that passed made it worse; made it more impossible. I never knew that if you did something you weren't particularly proud of . . . it became progressively difficult to undo it again." He did not comment on this. Simply continued to smoke, to watch her. "You said a great many letters. Who else did you hear from?"

"Well, I heard from Marcus, of course. That was business. And than a rather stilted, formal affair from Robert Morrow. Saying that he'd been here to see some play or other, and had had a drink with you and Christopher. I couldn't gather, however, whether he had come specifically to see the play or to see you."

"Yes. Well . . ."

"As soon as we realised that you were still alive and apparently occupied and with no intention of visiting us, Melissa and I set off in our coloured aeroplane for Mexico where we stayed with a mad old film star who lives in a house full of parakeets. Then, yesterday, we flew back to Queenstown, and what should I find waiting for me but yet another letter."

"From Robert?"

"No. From Christopher."

She could not help it. "From *Christopher*?"

"He must be an exceptionally talented young man. A London production, so soon, with so little experience. Of course, I always knew that he'd make a flagrant success of his life. Either that or end up in prison . . ."

But even this provocation could not divert her. "You mean *Christopher*? Wrote to *you*?"

"Said in that tone of voice, it sounds insulting."

"But why?"

"One can only imagine that he felt mildly responsible."

"But . . ." An idea was forming. A suspicion so wonderful that, if it was not true, then it must be scotched immediately. "But you didn't come home because of that letter? You came home to paint. To go back to Porthkerris and paint again?"

"Well, of course, taking the long view, I have. Mexico was inspiring. They have an extraordinary pink that keeps recurring in their buildings, and their pictures, and their very clothes . . ."

"Perhaps you'd had enough of Queenstown, and America," she persisted. "You've never been much good at staying in any one place for more than a couple of months. And, of course, you'll have to see Marcus. And start thinking about a new exhibition."

He stared at her blankly. "Why this catalogue of motives?"

"Well, there has to be some reason."

"I've just told you. I came to see you."

She did not want the cigarette he had given her. She leaned forward and stubbed it out, and then clasped her hands in her lap, the palms pressed tight together, the fingers interlaced. Misinterpreting her silence, Ben looked aggrieved. "I don't think, Emma, that you quite understand the situation. I literally flew in from Mexico, read Christopher's letter, kissed Melissa goodbye and flew out again. Didn't even have time to change my shirt. I then subjected myself to another twelve hours of flying, the tedium broken only by a series of uneatable meals, all of which tasted like

169

plastic. Do you think I endure such tortures simply to talk to Marcus Bernstein about another exhibition?"

"But, Ben . . ."

He was, however, well away, and in no mood to be interrupted.

"And, once arrived, do I go to Claridges, where Melissa has thoughtfully cabled in advance and reserved me a room? Do I indulge in a bath, or a drink, or a decent meal? No. I climb into the slowest taxi-cab this side of the Atlantic, and drive, through unspeakable rain, to Brookford" (he said the word as though it were something distasteful), "where, after interminable incorrect directions, I eventually run the Repertory theatre to earth. The taxi is at this moment outside, ticking up a monumental fare. And if you don't believe me, you can go and look."

"I believe you," said Emma, quickly.

"And then, when you do deign to appear, all you can talk about is Marcus Bernstein and some hypothetical exhibition. Do you know something? You're an ungrateful brat. A typical example of the modern generation. You don't deserve to have a father."

She said, "But I've been alone before. For years I've been alone. In Switzerland and Florence and Paris. You never came to see me then."

"You didn't need me then," said Ben flatly. "And I knew what you were doing, and who you were with. This time, when I read that letter from Christopher, I knew the first, faint stirrings of concern. Perhaps because Christopher, of all people, would never have written if he hadn't been concerned himself. Why didn't you tell me you'd met him in Paris?"

"I thought you wouldn't be pleased."

"It depends on what sort of a person he's turned into.

170

Has he changed very much from the small boy who lived with us at Porthkerris?"

"He looks the same . . . but he's tall . . . he's a man now. Single-minded and ambitious and, perhaps, a little self-centered. And with all the charm in the world." Talking about him, to Ben, was like having a weight lifted from her shoulders. Emma smiled. She said, "And I adore him."

Ben, accepting this, returned the smile. "You sound like Melissa, talking about Ben Litton. It seems that young Christopher and I have, after all, much in common. It's ironic that we should have wasted so many years in detesting each other. Perhaps I should make his acquaintance again. This time, we might get on a little better."

"Yes, I think you might."

"Melissa is joining me in a week or two. Coming down to Porthkerris."

"Living at the cottage?" said Emma, unbelieving.

Ben was amused. "Melissa? At the cottage? You must be joking. A suite has already been reserved at the Castle Hotel. I shall lead the life of a goldfish in a bowl, but perhaps, as I get older, the sybaritic existence is beginning to reveal its charms."

"But didn't she mind? Your coming home like that? Kissing her and leaving her without even taking time to change your shirt?"

"Emma, Melissa is a clever woman. She doesn't try to pin a man down or to possess him. She knows that the best way to hold on to someone you love is to . . . very gently . . . let him go. Women take a long time to learn this. Hester never did. How about you?"

"I'm learning," said Emma.

"The extraordinary thing is, I believe you are."

By now, darkness had fallen. This had happened, unheeded, while they talked, the dusk deepening impercepti-

171

bly until Ben's face, across the tiny distance that separated them, was simply a blur, his hair a wing of white. There was a lamp on the desk, but neither of them reached out to turn it on. The twilight enclosed them, the shut door kept the rest of the world out. They were the Littons; a family; together.

As they talked, the backstage shell of the theatre had rung with routine sounds. The last curtain call. Voices; Collins swearing at some unfortunate electrician. Hurrying feet, running upstairs to the dressing-rooms, anxious to be away, to be free of costumes and make-up, to catch buses, to go home, to cook food and wash stockings and, perhaps, to make love. Footsteps passed to and fro, in and out of the Green Room, *Darling, have you got a cigarette? Where's Delia? Has anybody seen Delia? There wasn't a phone call for me, was there?*

The sounds thinned out, as in twos and threes they left the theatre. Down the stone stairs, out of the banging door, into the narrow alley. A car started up. Somewhere a man started to whistle.

Behind Emma the door was abruptly opened, and the soft darkness split with an oblong of yellow light.

"Sorry to interrupt you . . ." It was Tommy Childers . . . "Wouldn't you like some illumination?" He snapped on the switch, and Ben and Emma were transfixed, blinking, like a couple of sleepy owls. "I just wanted something off my desk, before I go home."

Emma stood up, pulling her chair out of the way.

"Tommy, did you know this was my father?"

"I wasn't sure," said Tommy, smiling at Ben. "I thought you were in America."

"Everybody thought I was in America. Even my wife did until I said goodbye to her. I hope we haven't inconvenienced you, sitting here for so long in your office."

"Not at all. The only thing is the night-watchman's get-

ting a bit edgy about the stage door. I'll tell him you'll shut
it, Emma."

"Yes, of course."

"Well . . . Goodnight, Mr. Litton . . ."

Ben heaved himself to his feet. "I had thought of taking
Emma to London with me to-night. You wouldn't have any
objections to that?"

"None at all," said Tommy. "She's been working like a
slave for the past two weeks. Do her good to have a few days
off."

Emma said, "I don't know why you ask Tommy, when
you haven't even asked me."

"I don't ask you things," Ben said. "I tell you."

Tommy laughed. He said, "In that case, I expect you'll
be going to the first night."

Ben remained vague. "First night?"

Dryly, Emma enlightened him. "He means Christopher's private view. On Wednesday."

"So soon? I shall probably be back in Porthkerris by
then. We shall have to see."

"You should try and make it," said Tommy. They shook
hands. "It's been splendid meeting you. And Emma . . .
I'll see you sometime . . ."

"Maybe next week if *The Glass Door* folds up . . ."

"It won't," said Tommy. "If what Christo did to *Daisies
on the Grass* is anything to go by, it'll run as long as *The
Mousetrap*. Don't forget to shut the door."

He went away, downstairs; they heard his footsteps fade
down the alley below the window, out into the street. Emma
sighed, She said, "I think we should go. The night-watchman gets traumas if he thinks the place isn't properly locked
up. And that taxi driver of yours will either give up hope of
ever seeing you again, or else die of old age."

But Ben had once more settled himself into Tommy's

173

chair. "In a moment," he said. "There's just one more thing." He tapped a fresh cigarette from the American packet. "I wanted to ask you about Robert Morrow."

He had the most disconcertingly calm voice. It never changed or varied its inflections so that you were continuously being taken unawares. Every nerve in Emma's body leapt in warning, but she only said, casually enough, "What about him?"

"I always had a . . . strong feeling about that young man."

She tried being flippant. "You mean, apart from admiring the shape of his head."

He ignored this. "I asked you once if you liked him, and you said, 'I suppose so. I scarcely know him.'"

"What of it?"

"Do you know him any better now?"

"Well, yes, I suppose I do."

"When he came to Brookford that time, he wasn't simply visiting the theatre, was he? He came to see you."

"He came to find me. That isn't quite the same thing."

"But he took the trouble to find you. I wonder why."

"Perhaps he was prompted by the famous Bernstein sense of responsibility."

"Stop fencing."

"What do you want me to say?"

"I want you to tell me the truth. And to be honest with yourself."

"What makes you think I haven't?"

"Because a light has gone out of your eyes. Because I left you at Porthkerris, blooming and brown as a Gipsy. Because of the way you sit, the way you talk, the way you look." He lit the cigarette then, broke the match, and dropped it meticulously into the ash-tray. "Perhaps you forget I've been watching people, dissecting their personalities, painting them, for more years than you've been alive. And it's not Christopher who's made you unhappy. You've as good as told me that yourself."

"Perhaps it was you."

"Rubbish? A father? Angry, maybe. Hurt and resentful. Never heart-broken. Tell me about Robert Morrow. What went wrong?"

The little room was suddenly unbearably stuffy. Emma got up and went to the window, and opened it wide, leaning her elbow on the sill, and breathing in great draughts of cool, rain-washed air.

She said, "I suppose I never bothered to understand what sort of a person he really was."

"I don't understand."

"Well . . . meeting him, for the first time, the way I did. That started everything off on the wrong foot. I never thought of him as a person with a private life, and a private existence, and likes and dislikes . . . and lovers. He was just part of Bernstein's, as Marcus is part of Bernstein's. Simply there to look after us. To arrange exhibitions, and cash cheques and reserve hotel accommodation, and make sure that life, for the Littons, at least, runs on oiled wheels." She turned to frown at her father, puzzled by her own revelation. "How *could* I have been so moronic?"

"You probably inherited it from me. What put an end to this happy illusion?"

"Oh, I don't know. Things. He came down to Porthkerris to look at Pat Farnaby's pictures, and he asked me to go out to Gollan with him, because he didn't know the way. And it was raining, and very stormy, and he had a big thick sweater on, and we laughed about things. I don't know, but it was nice. And we were going to have dinner together, but he . . . well . . . anyway, I had a headache, so I didn't go after all. And then I came to Brookford to be with Christo,

and I didn't think about Robert Morrow any more until that
evening when he came to the theatre. I was clearing the
stage, and suddenly he spoke, just behind me, and I turned
round and he was there. And he had this girl with him. She's
called Jane Marshall, and she's an interior decorator, or
something very talented. She's pretty, and successful, and
they seemed so much a couple. Do you know what I mean?
Contained and self-sufficient and . . . together. And I felt
as though someone had slammed a door in my face and left
me out in the cold."

She turned from the window then, and came back to
the desk and sat on it, with her back to her father, and
picked up a rubber band and began to play with it, snapping
it like a catapult through her fingers.

"And they came back to the flat, for a beer or a coffee or
something, and everything was hideous, and Robert and I
had a horrible row, and he just walked out without saying
goodbye and took Jane Marshall with him. And drove back
to London, and, one imagines . . ." she tried desperately to
keep her voice light, ". . . lived happily ever after. Anyway,
I haven't seen him since."

"Is that why you wouldn't let Christopher tell him that
you were on your own?"

"Yes."

"Is he in love with this girl?"

"Christo thought he was. Christo thought she was gorgeous. He said that if Robert didn't marry her, he ought to
have his head examined."

"And what was the row about?"

Emma could scarcely remember. In retrospect, it jarred
as painfully as a gramophone record, played backwards, at
full pitch. An exchange of shouted words, meaningless, hurt-
ful, regretted.

"Oh, everything. You. And not answering your letter.

176

And Christo. I think he imagines Christo and I are madly in love, but by the time we'd got round to that I was so angry I didn't bother to disillusion him."

"Perhaps that was a mistake."

"Yes, perhaps it was."

"Do you want to stay here, at Brookford?"

"There's nowhere else to go."

"There's Porthkerris."

Emma turned to smile down at him. "With you? At the cottage?"

"Why not?"

"A thousand reasons. Running home to Daddy never solved anything. Besides, you can't run away from the inside of your own head."

He was on his way at last, and the self-delusion and the restlessness of the past six weeks were over. The Alvis—like a home-bound hunter—streamed west, out over the Hammersmith fly-over and onto the M.4. Robert settled her permanently in the fast outer lane, and kept her speedometer prudently, carefully down to seventy, for the frustration, at this stage, of being stopped by a police patrol would be almost more than he could bear. As he approached London Airport, the first rumble of thunder broke the heavy, quiet air, and he stopped in at the first lay-by and put up the hood. He was only just in time. As he moved out into the road again, the sullen evening erupted like a volcano. The wind, with staggering abruptness, swept up from the west, bearing towering black thunderheads before it, and when the rain came it was a positive explosion of water, sheets of it, like a monsoon downpour, against which the windscreen-wipers could scarcely compete. In seconds, the surface of the road was awash, reflecting the livid streaks of forked lightning which split the sky.

It occurred to him that perhaps it would be wise to stop, and wait until the worst of the storm was over, by now his sense of relief at doing what he had for weeks been subconsciously wanting to do, was stronger than any ideas of caution. So he went on, and the huge cambered curve of the motorway pouted up towards him, and roared beneath his wheels, and was flung away in a wave of water; already a thing of the past; rejected and forgotten, along with his own feeble uncertainties.

He found the theatre closed. By the light of the street lamp, he was able to read the posters. A MIDSUMMER NIGHT'S DREAM. Unlit, deserted, the place looked gloomy as the Mission Hall it had once been. The door was barred and bolted; all the windows dark.

He got out of the car. It was cooler now, and he reached into the back seat and took out a sweater that had been lying there since the Bosham week-end, and pulled it on over his shirt. He slammed the door shut, and then saw the solitary taxi, waiting at the pavement's edge, the driver slumped over his wheel. He might have been dead.

"Is there anyone in there?"

"Must be, Guv-nor. I'm waiting for a fare."

Robert walked down the pavement, as far as the narrow lane, down which, so long ago, Emma and Christopher had come, walking like lovers, with their arms about each other. On this side of the sombre building a first-floor window blazed with uncurtained light. He went down the shadowed alley, tripped over a dustbin, found an open door. Inside, a flight of stone stairs led upwards, illuminated palely from a light which burned on the first-floor landing. He was assailed by the stale theatre smell of grease-paint, oil-paint, musty velvet. From above came the murmur of voices and he went upstairs, towards it, and found the short passage, and the door marked PRODUCER'S OFFICE, ajar, and edged with bright light.

He pushed the door open and the voices ceased abruptly, and he found himself on the threshold of a tiny, crowded office, looking down into the astonished faces of Ben and Emma Litton.

Emma sat on the desk, with her back to her father, facing Robert. She wore a short dress, cut simply as an overall, and her long legs were bare and brown. The room was so small that as he stood there in the doorway, he was only an arm's length from her. If he wanted he could reach out and touch her. He thought that she had never looked so beautiful.

His relief and pleasure at seeing Emma was so great that the unexpectedness of Ben Litton's appearance became insignificant. Ben himself was equally unsurprised. He simply raised his dark eyebrows and said:

"Well, bless my soul, see who's turned up now."

Robert put his hands in his pockets, and said, "I thought . . ."

Ben held up a hand. "I know. You thought I was in America. Well, I'm not; I'm in Brookford. And the sooner I get out of the place and back to London, the better."

"But when did you . . . ?"

But Ben was stubbing out his cigarette, standing up, ruthlessly interrupting. "You didn't by any chance notice a taxi-cab at the front of the theatre, did you?"

"Yes, I did. The driver looked as though he had become fossilised to the wheel."

"Poor fellow. I must go and put his mind at rest."

"I've got my car," said Robert. "If you like I'll drive you back to London."

"Even better. I can pay the man off." Emma had not

moved. Now, Ben edged his way around the desk, and Robert stood aside to let him out of the door.

"By the way, Robert, Emma's coming too. Will you have room for her?"

"But of course."

In the doorway, they eyed each other. Then Ben gave a satisfied nod. "Splendid," he said. "I'll wait outside for you both."

"Did you know he was coming?"

Emma shook her head.

"Did it have anything to do with the letter Christopher wrote to him?"

Emma nodded.

"He flew back, to-day, from the States, to make sure you were all right?"

Emma nodded again, her eyes shining. "He'd been in Mexico with Melissa. But he came straight here. Even Marcus doesn't know he's in the country. He didn't even go to London. He took a taxi from the airport to Brookford. And he wasn't angry about Christopher, and he says if I want I can go back to Porthkerris with him."

"And are you?"

"Oh, Robert, I can't go on, all my life, making the same mistakes. And it was Hester's mistake, too. We both wanted Ben to conform to our ideas of a nice reliable husband, and a kind domestic father. And it was as realistic as trying to cage a panther. And when you came to think of it, how dull caged panthers are! Besides, Ben isn't my problem any longer. He's Melissa's."

Robert said, "So what price now, coming at the bottom of a long list of priorities?"

Emma made a face at him. "You know, Ben once said that you had a noble head, and that you should grow a beard and then he would paint you. But if I tried to paint you it would be with a great big balloon coming out of your mouth with I TOLD YOU SO written on it."

"I never said that to anyone in the whole of my life. And I certainly didn't come all the way down here tonight to say it."

"What did you come to say?"

"That if I'd known you were on your own, I'd have been here weeks ago. That if I can get two seats for Christo's first night, I want you to come with me. That I'm sorry about shouting at you, that last time I was here."

"I shouted too."

"I hate having rows with you, but in some extraordinary way, being away from you is a thousand times worse. I kept telling myself that it was simply something that was over, and best forgotten. But all the time you were never out of the back of my mind. Jane knew. She told me this evening, she'd known all along."

"Jane . . . ?"

"I'm ashamed to say I've been running Jane round in demented circles trying to keep myself from squaring up to the horrible truth."

"But it was because of Jane that I made Christopher promise not to ring you up. I thought . . ."

"And it was because of Christopher that I didn't come back to Brookford."

"You thought we were having an affair, didn't you?"

"Wasn't that what I was meant to think?"

"But you silly man, Christopher's my brother."

Robert took her head between his hands, and put his thumbs beneath her chin and turned her face up to his. Just before he kissed her, he said, "And how the hell was I supposed to know that?"

* * *

When they got back to the car, there was no sign of Ben, but he had left a message for them, tucked between the windscreen wiper and the wind-shield. "Like a parking ticket," said Emma.

It was an unconventional letter, written on a sheet of cartridge paper torn from Ben's sketch book, and headed by two thumb-nail sketches—two profiles turned to face each other. There was no mistaking her own determined chin and Robert's formidable nose.

"It's us. It's for both of us. Read it aloud."

Robert did so. *"The cabby seemed morose at the thought of returning to London on his own, so I decided to accompany him. I shall be at Claridges, but would prefer not to be disturbed before noon to-morrow."*

"But if I'm not to go to Claridges before noon, where am I meant to go?"

"You're meant to come home with me. To Milton Gardens."

"But I haven't any things. I haven't even got a toothbrush."

"I will buy you a toothbrush," said Robert, and kissed her, and then went on reading the letter. *"By then I should have caught up on my sleep and had time to cool the champagne, and will be ready to celebrate anything you may have to tell me."*

"The wily old brute! He knew, all along."

"My love, and God bless you both. Ben."

After a little, Emma said, "Is that all?"

"Not quite." He handed her the letter and Emma saw, beneath Ben's signature, a third little drawing. A wing of white hair, a brown face, a pair of dark and cruelly observant eyes.

"Self-portrait," said Robert. "Ben Litton by Ben Litton.

It must be unique. One day, we might sell it for thousands of pounds."

My love and God bless you both.

"I shan't ever want to sell it," said Emma.

"Nor I. Come on, my darling, it's time to go home."